THE DEATH OF
COMRADE PRESIDENT

ALSO BY ALAIN MABANCKOU

African Psycho

Broken Glass

Memoirs of a Porcupine

Black Bazaar

Tomorrow I'll Be Twenty

The Lights of Pointe-Noire

Black Moses

THE DEATH OF COMRADE PRESIDENT

A Novel

ALAIN MABANCKOU

Translated by Helen Stevenson

THE
NEW
PRESS

NEW YORK
LONDON

Requests for permission to reproduce selections from this book
should be made through our website: https://thenewpress.com/contact.

Originally published in French as *Les cigognes sont immortelles* ©
Editions du Seuil, 2018
First published in Great Britain by Serpent's Tail,
an imprint of Profile Books Ltd, 2020
Published in the United States by The New Press, New York, 2020
Distributed by Two Rivers Distribution

ISBN 978-1-62097-607-4 (ebook)

LIBRARY OF CONGRESS CATALOGING-IN-PUBLICATION DATA

Names: Mabanckou, Alain, 1966– author. | Stevenson, Helen (Translator), translator.
Title: The death of Comrade President : a novel / Alain Mabanckou ; translated by
    Helen Stevenson.
Other titles: Cigognes sont immortelles. English
Description: New York : The New Press, 2020. | Originally published in France as
    Les cigognes sont immortelles by Éditions du Seuil, Paris, in 2018. | Summary:
    "A novel telling the story of Michel, whose life is overthrown when, in March 1977,
    just before the arrival of the rainy season, Congo's Comrade President Marien
    Ngouabi is brutally murdered"—Provided by publisher.
Identifiers: LCCN 2020006734 | ISBN 9781620976067 (hardback) | ISBN
    9781620976074 (ebook)
Subjects: LCSH: Congo (Brazzaville)—History—1960—Fiction. | LCGFT: Novels.
Classification: LCC PQ3989.2.M217 C5413 2020 | DDC 843/.914—dc23
LC record available at https://lccn.loc.gov/2020006734

The New Press publishes books that promote and enrich public discussion and
understanding of the issues vital to our democracy and to a more equitable world.
These books are made possible by the enthusiasm of our readers; the support of a
committed group of donors, large and small; the collaboration of our many partners
in the independent media and the not-for-profit sector; booksellers, who often
hand-sell New Press books; librarians; and above all by our authors.

www.thenewpress.com

Printed in the United States of America

2   4   6   8   10   9   7   5   3   1

In memory of my mother Pauline Kengué,
my father Roger Kimangou
and my uncle René Mabanckou

for the Captain
and for the Immortal

and all the cranes that fly overhead

THE DEATH OF
COMRADE PRESIDENT

Saturday 19 March 1977

Our plot

Maman Pauline says you should always wear clean clothes when you go out. She says the main thing people criticise is what you're wearing; you can hide the rest, dirty underwear, for example, or socks with holes in.

So I've just changed my shirt and shorts.

Papa Roger is sitting under the mango tree, at the far end of our plot, busy listening to our national radio station, the Voice of the Congolese Revolution, which since yesterday afternoon has broadcast nothing but Soviet music.

Without turning round to look at me, he gives me my orders:

'Michel, don't dawdle on the way! Don't forget your mother's errands, my red wine, my tobacco, and don't lose my change!'

He reminds me not to dawdle because I have a habit of stopping to drool over the cars of the black capitalists near the Avenue of Independence, as though I'll never get another chance. I just stand there gazing at them, imagining one day I'll buy one myself, I'll hide it at night in a lock-up, guarded by bulldogs I've dosed with Johnnie Walker Red Label mixed with corn spirit to make them ten times more vicious than even the dogs that belong to the whites in the town centre. I get caught up in my thoughts, and forget all about Maman

Pauline's errands; I forget Papa Roger asked me for red wine and the tobacco powder he stuffs up his nostrils, making his eyes water.

My father's concerned about his change, too, because ever since primary school I've had a bit of a problem: often the pockets of my shorts have holes in, from hiding bits of wire in them for fixing the holes in my plastic shoes, in case they fall apart right there in the street. So, instead of pocketing the change I clutch it tightly in my right hand. Unfortunately, whenever I wave hello to the local mums and dads (which you have to do, or they'll go and say crazy things to my parents), the money just falls on to the ground. I have to pick it up pretty smart, or the young guys smoking pot on street corners will snatch it to buy presents for those skinny girls, the *runaways*, that hang around with them. It's their own fault we call them the *runaways*: they've left their parents' homes, they dress like they're not wearing any clothes, you can see everything, they don't care, and they'll do things with any boy that I won't go into here, or they'll go round saying Michel always exaggerates, and sometimes he says rude things without meaning to ...

Before I leave our plot, I take a good look back at it. There's barbed wire all round it. The entrance is just four planks knocked together, with gaps so we can see who wants to come in. Just to confuse Maman Pauline and Papa Roger, I used to slip between the barbed wire, first one leg, then the other, and slip out without hurting myself, to go down to the River Tchinouka with my friends to hunt swallows and weaver birds. But that was all back when I was at primary school, and now I'm at Three-Glorious-Days middle school I'm allowed out through the door.

It was Maman Pauline who bought this plot, and she gave her little brother, Uncle Mompéro, the task of building us a house. It cost too much to build a permanent house, so ours is just made of wood. Pontenegrins call this type of house 'houses in waiting'. I don't like that expression. There are loads of families round here who wanted to show they had money, so started out building proper houses, but never put in the famous windows that keep the noise out, because they cost too much. Surely they're the families with 'houses in waiting'. At least ours is actually finished, there's nothing more to add, it's made out of okumé boards, with a roof of corrugated iron and plywood windows. We have two bedrooms: one for me, one for Maman Pauline and Papa Roger. In my parents' room there's a smell of mothballs, 24/7. The smell gets rid of roaches and other kinds of insect that mess up the wax-print fabrics my mother's *pagne* wrappers are made from. The bed is very tidily made, thanks to Papa Roger, who copies the technique of the chambermaids in the Victory Palace Hotel where he works. Papa Roger's well in with his boss at the hotel, Madame Ginette: it's unusual for someone to stay in a hotel job for twenty years without stealing the nice tablecloths or the sheets that come from Europe.

In the bedrooms at the Victory Palace Hotel, the sheets are all white. Maman Pauline doesn't want that at home, she thinks white is for the corpses in the morgue at the Adolphe-Cissé hospital, so she uses her own brightly coloured prints instead. The thing I like about their bed is the big pillows and the designs my mother's knitted for them: two birds kissing with their beaks, the big one's Papa Roger, the smaller one's Maman Pauline herself. You're bound to sleep well with pillows like that. I know other people who have lions or panthers on theirs, the idea being they eat up pests like snakes and scorpions but really it's the people sleeping in them who get eaten up in their dreams instead.

Since we only have two rooms, things get pretty complicated when members of the family from our village pitch up in Pointe-Noire with nowhere to stay. You can't shut the door on them, you can't just say you don't know them, so we put them up in the living room on mats, because if they sleep in proper beds they'll only get uppity and start saying it's their house now, and they'll stay till their dying day. Also, if Maman Pauline and Papa Roger die before they do, they'll kick me out and inherit everything.

In the living room we have a really wobbly table. My mother says it's a bit disabled, it's got a poorly leg. My job is to stabilise the leg, with two little stones, when important people come to eat at our house. I keep the stones hidden in a cupboard by the window; it's the only piece of furniture we inherited two years ago when my Uncle Albert Moukila who worked for the National Electricity Board died. Our relatives who had come from the village for the funeral all made a dash for Maman Pauline's older brother's property; they told my cousins to leave the new house their father had built for them in the Comapon neighbourhood and find somewhere else with their mother's family. He was a very nice uncle; he arranged free electricity for anyone from our ethnic group who lived near his house, near the quartier Rex. We lived too far away; Uncle Albert, now deceased, couldn't get a cable from there to our place in Voungou to give us free lighting. That's OK; the main reason we don't have electricity is because Voungou is still a new neighbourhood. The Vili's cemeteries used to be here, the tribe that live by the Côte Sauvage and eat sharks, though there are plenty of other smaller fish in the sea. The traditional chiefs of the Vili knocked down their pretty cemeteries and sold off the plots without even consulting the dead, but it was good news for anyone who couldn't afford to buy land in the other neighbourhoods of Pointe-Noire, the ones where the members of the Congolese Party of Labour live, with their big bellies and shiny bald heads.

Our kitchen is outside, but attached to the house, like a child on its mother's back. The toilets are opposite, well away from the kitchen, in case bad smells get into whatever's cooking and spoil our appetite. Besides, they don't really deserve to be called toilets. It's just four sheets of metal Uncle Mompéro put up to stop passers-by from watching us from the street. If I want a pee, or something more substantial – which I won't go into detail about here, or people will say Michel always goes over the top and that sometimes he says rude things without meaning to – I have to take a bucketful of water and pour it down so that the next person won't know what's gone on before. But I have to be pretty careful, if I make a mess pouring the water it splashes on my feet and the flies will be after me for the whole of the rest of the day.

The Malongas and the Mindondos

I go past the Malongas' place. Monsieur Malonga's three wives always cook outside, in the middle of their plot. If anyone criticises them, Monsieur Malonga just says that back in the day their Lari ancestors' food was always prepared outside on three stones placed in a triangle, and it was all fine, the dishes even tasted better.

The Malonga children, all eleven of them, have the job of making sure the fire doesn't go out. If they fail, their mothers won't fill their plates up when it's time to eat. Kékélé, the oldest brother, is twelve, he'll be taking his Primary School Certificate this year, he has a different teacher to the one I had when I was in that class last year, he's got Monsieur Ngakala Bitekoutekou, who's not very nice, he whips the pupils because he wanted to go and teach in the north of our country but the State refused his request and sent him to us in the south to show there was no tribalism in the Congo these days, it's all just the imperialist Europeans trying to divide us.

The Malongas aren't black capitalists; their father sometimes comes round for a chat with Papa Roger under the mango tree. They don't speak the same language, in our family we're Bembés and speak the Bembé language, but either the Malongas speak the language of Pointe-Noire, Munukutuba, or they speak in French, but Monsieur Malonga's French is nothing like as good as my father's. For instance, one day my father used the word *symposium*. Monsieur Malonga was open-mouthed, the word was completely new to his ears, he'd never even heard it before.

'*Symposium*, what's that? Really, Roger, sometimes you come out with words even the whites don't have in their dictionaries!'

Monsieur Malonga works in the depot of the Printania store in the town centre, next to the Victory Palace Hotel. Because of his work he has things that come direct from France, that smell of France and are sold at Printania for loads of money. But Monsieur Malonga also has another job at weekends and it's this second job he's famous for in our neighbourhood. Families bring their boys to him and he makes personalised fetishes for them, so they'll be good fighters. The most powerful fetish is called the *kamon*. Monsieur Malonga makes little cuts on the boy's wrists with a Gillette razor blade, then rubs some powder into the wounds (a mixture of lots of ground-up things, like viper's tooth, gorilla hairs, lantana leaves and bee's sting). After that Monsieur Malonga makes this great show with an empty bottle, which he whacks against the child's head. The child feels nothing, but the bottle breaks into a thousand pieces against his skull. Which means that when the boy headbutts someone, the other guy will see a thousand stars and pass out.

Monsieur Malonga learned these secrets in his village, Mplangala, where he goes once a month. That's where he gets his viper's teeth and gorilla hairs. You can get hold of lantana leaves or bee sting in the new neighbourhoods of Pointe-Noire, or behind Mont-Kamba cemetery, where there's still a bit of bush left here and there, with domestic animals who've decided they've had enough of being human slaves and want to go wild again.

Girls can't have the *kamon*, no boy will ever marry them if they do, they'd be too scared of getting beaten up, and losing face in the neighbourhood. I really wanted Monsieur Malonga to do the *kamon* on me, but to my great regret Maman Pauline and Papa Roger refused, because of the bad behaviour of one boy called Claver Ngoutou-Nziété. Monsieur Malonga had made him really strong, everyone avoided him, and he had no one to try out his *kamon* on. So he turned on his own parents, one head-butt for his mother, another for his father, both of them ended up in the emergency room at Adolphe-Cissé hospital. When my mother heard about this terrible business on the radio, she went and told Monsieur Malonga that it was unacceptable, that her boy Michel was never going to have the *kamon*, no way, and that if he gave it to me in secret when I went to see his children she would report it to the Voungou police, and he shouldn't forget, the chief of police was from the same ethnic group as us …

Just beyond the Malongas' house is the Mindondos'. They built a proper, solid house, and their plot has concrete walls round it. They have swings and bicycles and new toys and a big blue tub for their children, who go round boasting that they've got a swimming pool, but I've seen the pool at the Victory Palace Hotel so I know a real swimming pool is way bigger and you can swim up and down in it, or jump into it off a board and go splash! in the water. When you've finished you take a white towel and wipe yourself with it a bit and then wrap it round your waist, then go and lie down on a plastic lounger and read books with nice, simple stories in them. The Mindondos can't swim up and down and they can't jump off a board and go splash! in the water. They just sit around their tub and throw plastic ducks into it while pretending they're real live ducks.

The door to the Mindondos' lot is very fine, made of ebony wood, with a little hole you can open and shut so you can get a look at someone before opening up. They know some people are just greedy so-and-sos who'll claim they simply happened to be passing and wanted to say hi to the children. They're just opportunists, who don't realise that black capitalists carefully count the number of mouths to be fed. If you turn up at their house they get all anxious about how long you're going to stay, in case there are too many mouths at the meal table. This is why Monsieur Mindondo leaves magazines in the living room for visitors to read and look at the nice photos, while he and his family are eating.

Monsieur Mindondo is a member of the Congolese Party of Labour. He studied in the USSR for five years. He wanted to bring back a wife from there, but his parents threatened him:

'If you get yourself a white wife we'll put a curse on you; you'll never have children with her, or you'll have children with snouts and boars' feet! We'll choose for you, from the Kamba people, a nice round, short woman, not one of those tall thin white women who look like they eat nothing but macaroni!'

The wife they found for him is round and short, that's Madame Léopoldine Mindondo. She never says hi to the local mamas, and avoids them by doing her shopping at Printania with the whites and other black capitalists.

I know all the Mindondo children by name; they're the only family in Pointe-Noire with such grand names. The big brother is called Thomas Aquinas Mindondo, then there are three other boys: Dionysus Mindondo, Olympus Mindondo and Poseidon Mindondo. They only have one daughter, Artemis Mindondo, but she's still crawling around on all fours.

The big brother, Thomas Aquinas Mindondo, is fourteen, but he doesn't go to our school, the Three-Glorious-Days, he goes to the French school, Charlemagne, with the children of the whites and the black capitalists who come to our neighbourhood whenever Monsieur Mindondo celebrates one of his children's birthdays.

When Monsieur Mindondo has guests who wear ties, his colleagues from the Congolese Party of Labour, they park their cars all over the place, even outside our lot. Monsieur Mindondo's already had a run-in with Papa Roger, who'd asked him to stop letting these guys in ties park outside our house, because some people might think it was our car, that we've suddenly turned into black capitalists. Old Mindondo didn't even hear the end of my father's remark about black capitalists, he thought Papa Roger was criticising his car because it wasn't French or Japanese, it was a Volvo 343, so he couldn't have bought it at the CFAO in the rue Côte-Matève where my Uncle René is a big boss, in charge of lots of people. Monsieur Mindondo said Papa Roger was just a poor little hotel receptionist, who'd never be able to buy a Volvo 343. Maman Pauline waded in and yelled at Madame Léopoldine Mindondo, who'd called her an ignorant banana seller. She also added that my mother only had one child, and the child wasn't even a girl, just a lazy boy child, who spent his whole time daydreaming, writing things down on pieces of paper, as though roaches were fighting in his brain. That's me, Michel. Also, again according to Madame Léopoldine Mindondo, the reason I'd never had to repeat a year since I'd been in primary school was nothing to do with intelligence, but because Madame Pauline had greased the palms of the teachers, male and female, and of the head of the school too, and would grease the palms of the teachers at the Three-Glorious-Days the same, and after that at the Karl

Marx Lycée. What hurt my mother most was when Madame Léopoldine Mindondo said that if her son Michel – that's me – died tomorrow, my mother would be all alone, and everyone would say she was a witch and had given her only child to the spirits in exchange for supernatural powers and worldly success. In fact, what Madame Léopoldine Mindondo meant was that the only reason my mother's business had been doing so well for years was because she used her *gris-gris* to bewitch the customers and that she'd happily sacrifice me to the spirits to make herself even more money.

Maman Pauline had not appreciated these accusations. That evening, she said to me, in front of Papa Roger, who seemed to agree with her:

'Michel, do me a big favour: if you see that imbecile Thomas Aquinas in the street, give him a thump!'

I said I would, just to calm her down. Thomas Aquinas already has the muscles of a black African sportsman. He plays sport with real machines at the French school, Charlemagne. He's been picked for the Kioulou regional athletics championships and Papa Roger had shown me his photo in *La Semaine*, with a huge headline: 'Thomas Aquinas Mindondo, the great hope of Pontenegrin athletics.'

If she wanted me to do her this big favour, I felt like asking her why she had forbidden Monsieur Malonga to make me a *kamon* …

Case by Case

Here's Ma Moubobi's shop, Case by Case, just off the Avenue of Independence. It's pretty untidy and really small, and smells of salt fish and peanut butter. There are no set prices; it depends on whether or not you know Ma Moubobi, that's why the shop's called Case by Case.

Papa Roger and Maman Pauline do know Ma Moubobi. Me too – that's me, Michel: she sees me every week in her shop, and I went to primary school with Olivier Moubobi, her only child, like I'm Maman Pauline's only child. They used to make fun of him because he was always late, and the teacher would tell him to kneel down in the corner for an hour. When he was allowed back to his seat he'd sleep, and as soon as he started to snore the teacher would grab him by the ear and drag him back into the corner, and he had to stay there on his knees until the end of lessons. Ma Moubobi took him out of school for good, so they'd stop teasing him. Before that she'd created mayhem right through the school. She'd insulted everyone, including the head teacher. She and her son threw stones everywhere, and we all ran around like crazy trying to avoid getting hit in the face by a stone and ending up in the emergency room at Adolphe-Cissé.

Ma Moubobi was yelling:

'I'm gonna put a jinx on you! I'm gonna put a jinx on you! Hey, look at me!'

She lifted her *pagne* to show something I'm not going to go into here, or people will say Michel always exaggerates, and sometimes he says rude things without meaning to … We closed our eyes, because it's serious stuff, seeing a *maman* in her bare skin, you could easily have to repeat the year because of a jinx like that.

Ma Moubobi had vanished with Olivier Moubobi, and that was the last time we saw him in class.

For a while now, Olivier's been hanging out in his mother's shop. He won't even talk to me these days. He says I was one of the kids he had to leave school because of, and if he'd stayed he'd be like me, one of the best pupils in the Kouilou region, and already have his Primary School Certificate and be at Three-Glorious-Days and be going on to the Karl Marx Lycée after he'd taken the Intermediate Studies diploma.

Maman Pauline says I mustn't go round saying that Ma Moubobi is gross and sits snoring by her counter when there are no customers in her shop. You don't choose to be like that; sometimes you get fat from an illness you're born with, or because evil spirits are jealous of how much money you earn. Ma Moubobi manages very well on her own, even without a husband, that's why the jealous spirits have landed her with fatness and snoring instead of giving it to the bad people.

We only go and do little shops at Case by Case, when we've run out of something. We could go to the Grand Marché, but it's too far, you have to wait for the bus over the Voungou Bridge, and beyond the Fond Tié-Tié crossroads. The bus goes straight on then turns right further on, at the Mawata round-about. The driver mustn't get it wrong or he'll end up in Fouks or Makaya-Makaya, when he was meant to be making for the

Trois-Cents, Rex and Duo neighbourhoods, on past the West Africans' mosque till he gets to the Grand Marché. It's too complicated, especially as on the way there he has to swerve round the potholes in the Avenue Moe-Prat, and watch out for the tramps at the crossroads of the Boulevard Félix-Tchicaya and the Avenue Alphonse-Demosso. They cross the road without looking left or right, like sheep blindly following the one in front, so that when one of them stupidly plunges into a ditch the whole flock stupidly plunges into the ditch after it.

Anyway, if you want to go to the Grand Marché you'd best not be in a hurry and get into one of the so-called fula-fula buses. They pull up at every bus stop even when they're already full, the conductor's job is to yell at the top of his voice and force people on, without warning them there's no room left and they'll be stuck together like sardines. It's hot in there, the passengers are all sweating like they've got taps running from their armpits. Some people from Voungou prefer the two-hour walk, and not because they haven't got the money for the fula-fula ticket, just to avoid getting drenched with the sweat of people they don't know and who maybe only ever wash accidently, when it's raining …

Ma Moubobi is sitting behind her counter, which isn't a real one, she's just put two barrels side by side with a plank of okumé between them, and lots of packets of Kojak sweets. It's her technique for attracting children. And if their parents won't buy them any, the kids roll around on the floor crying, moaning that they've got stomach ache and Ma Moubobi's Kojak sweets are the only cure.

Salted fish hang from the ceiling on strings of elastic. When there's a draught from outside, the fish swing from side to side, just centimetres from Ma Moubobi's head. And if someone wants to buy one, she raises her arm, catches a fish by its tail, and tugs hard. The elastic goes ping! and the fish drops down on to the okumé board!

Ma Moubobi grabs it and sniffs.

'Hmm, not gone off yet …What will you give me?'

She starts arguing about the price with the customer, then ends up saying:

'OK, never mind, your price is my price, but just so as you know, I'll make nothing from it, I'm only doing it for your children, not for you …'

Behind Ma Moubobi, on the wall of the building, there's a framed photo of Comrade President Marien Ngouabi. When you promise to pay her by the end of the month, Ma Moubobi turns round and points at the president's portrait.

'You'd better pay by the date we agreed, as Comrade President Marien Ngouabi's my witness …'

The customer looks at the photo of our leader of the Congolese Socialist Revolution with respect and fear. It's the same one we had in our classroom at primary school. Comrade President Marien Ngouabi is wearing a military cap and is looking away to his right. His military jacket is magnificent, the top button's fastened, and just above his right-hand pocket is the badge of the para-commandos, which proves he can jump from a helicopter or a plane and land on the ground without breaking his skull, thanks to his parachute. Comrade President Marien Ngouabi looks sad in this photo. Maybe it's dawned on him that it's not easy being a leader of the Revolution in a country where people all want to pay later.

The customers are convinced that Comrade President Ngouabi is in the shop, watching them, and they just can't not pay their debts on time when a president's witnessed them taking their goods without getting their money out …

I'm in the queue behind three grown-up men.

The first one has paid for his two tins of sardines and left.

The second one places a soursap, a pineapple and a packet of manioc flour on the counter and gets some money out of his pocket to pay.

The third one hasn't picked up anything; he's just holding us all up, chit-chatting away with Ma Moubobi, asking her where Olivier is.

Ma Moubobi's really happy someone's interested in her son.

'Oh, Olivier? Thank God, he's got a job on a fula-fula bus now, he's a conductor. I told his boss he'd better not push my son around, or he'll find me undressing in front of his bus and all his passengers!'

And they both laugh. I can't see what's funny about it myself. It reminds me of the day Ma Moubobi stripped off in our school and I tried not to see her naked form, because of the jinx that would have come down on me and stopped me getting my Primary School Certificate and going on to Three-Glorious-Days.

I don't know what this gossipy guy is whispering in Ma Moubobi's ear, she keeps bursting out laughing and patting her hair. Is she falling in love with him or is he chatting her up to get some free produce?

Ma Moubobi finally sees me standing behind the guy chatting her up when the second customer's finished paying and walks out.

'Who's this then? Pauline Kengué's boy! So, are you going to lose your parents' change again today?'

The chatty guy turns round and jeers:

'Look at you, boy! Well, well! Just look at yourself! Aren't you ashamed? Olivier's your age and he's already working on a fula-fula, he'll be a full-time conductor soon, and you turn up in Ma Moubobi's shop dressed like that? Have you no respect, or is that just the fashion now?'

I examine myself from top to toe: my shirt's on backwards! I take a step back, to leave the shop, but the chatty man's arm shoots out and catches me by the shoulder.

'Go behind Ma Moubobi's counter and put your shirt on properly!'

Ma Moubobi closes her eyes while I change my shirt round. The man closes his eyes too, even though we're the same sex.

I put my shirt back on right, and come out to line up behind the chatty man.

'You go first, my boy, I'll be here for a while, I haven't finished telling Ma Moubobi about when I—'

He stops short, looks me up and down again.

'You doing it on purpose, boy? You haven't done up your bottom button. Trying to show us all your great big belly button?'

I do up the button, rather annoyed at him saying I have a big belly button. Still, it'll teach me to go round criticising Ma Moubobi for being fat and snoring.

It's my turn at the till now. I can't find the money I had in my hand. Ma Moubobi waves a five thousand CFA franc note with no creases in it, as though someone had washed it and ironed it with a smoothing iron to keep it clean and flat.

'It fell on the floor while you were putting your shirt on properly ...'

Now I can breathe again. I was already imagining what Papa Roger would say. I say a prayer that Ma Moubobi won't mention this to my father. I can't count on her, she tells everyone everything, her mouth has no stop button, that's what they say about her at Voungou, that's why she hasn't had a husband since Olivier's father, who left her before the child could even walk.

She gives me a large packet. I glance inside at the contents: I see Maggi stock cubes, palm oil and peanut butter. It's Maman Pauline's order, but there are still some things missing. Before I can ask her, Ma Moubobi says:

'Look carefully, I've put your father's wine and tobacco right at the bottom. The change is in a little bag inside …'

Bad mood

Maman Pauline is home already, and I get the feeling she's really cross. She snatches the bag of shopping from me. She rummages inside, hands me back the bottle of wine and Papa Roger's tobacco and keeps the rest.

I know it's not because of us she's in a bad mood. Things probably went wrong wherever she went first thing this morning, when the lorries from the Pointe-Noire highway collect the bins outside the houses of the black capitalists and pretend not to notice if there's rubbish outside the plots of people like the Malongas and the rest of us.

My mother had left us clear instructions: we must start boiling the pork at ten o'clock on the dot, so that when she got back she'd only have to add the things I'd just bought at Ma Mouboubi's shop.

Every weekend she goes to ask some of the shopkeepers for the money they've owed her for months. She can't really force them to pay, because these women are friends she drinks Primus with in the bars at the Grand Marché. Besides, many of them come from the same village as her, Louboulou. They all played together there as children, went to fetch water from the stream, badmouthing the boys who tried to do things with them that I can't go into here or people will say Michel's always exaggerating, sometimes he even says rude things without meaning to. So the shopkeepers take advantage of Maman Pauline's kindness. Papa Roger's always telling her off, saying she'll never make any profit, when she actually needs a lot of money to buy bananas in bulk from the peasants in Les Bandas, and pay the young guys who transport them to the station at Loubomo, and reserve a whole freight car of the Congo-Ocean railway, and hand over lots of ten thousand CFA franc notes to the people who load the produce into the train, then later on to the people who take it off at the station in Pointe-Noire, and finally also to the people who transport it to the Grand Marché. Sometimes she's unlucky, the train derails and the CO railway informs her that they can't compensate her for her bananas because it's a case of '*force majeure*', which, as Papa Roger explained to me, means that no one could have known in advance that the train would be derailed. Now everyone knows that derailments happen all the time at Dolisie, Dechavanne, Mont Bélo, Hamon and Baratier stations. Trains can get stuck there for ten to fifteen days before the European technicians arrive from Brazzaville in a handcar and fix the tracks. They're wily ones, these white technicians, they hide their technique from our railway workers, so they'll get lots of money, when all they're doing is giving orders to the Congolese who lug huge stones around in the hot sun, lay tracks and tighten bolts with no gloves on their hands. When there are derailments, Maman Pauline hands out her bananas to the CO railway workers, otherwise the wild animals will eat them. Some passengers try to give her money, but she refuses, she says it's fine, she'll have better luck next time. And the conductors, who are completely and utterly without shame, help themselves, as though the bananas were a gift from the CO railway. But since it's obvious at a glance how nice my mother is to their clients, who rudely stuff themselves silly, without a word of thanks, they promise her that next time she travels she'll go first class, along with the whites and the black capitalists, on condition she keeps her mouth shut in front of the other shopkeepers, because there aren't enough seats in the carriage, the only one in the whole Micheline with air conditioning. Even if she accepts her air-conditioned present, it's nothing like the value of the produce she lost through the derailment. And when she comes home empty-handed she's pretty grumpy with us, and really tired from her long, fruitless journey, and she sits down next to Papa Roger in the living room and watches him do long, complicated sums on pieces of paper until my father, looking very concerned, throws the Biro down on the table in front of him and says:

'It's no good, Pauline …You know, I can help you at the end of the month with my salary from the hotel.'

My mother is too proud, she refuses Papa Roger's helping hand, and he worries a lot, because it's hard to eat or sleep well if you have money problems. It was the same proud streak that drove her to buy our plot and have our house built. She didn't want to be like the other women in Pointe-Noire who just expect their husbands to pay for everything, even sewing needles or threads for weaving in their hair. Maman Pauline is so proud, she promises Papa Roger every time that she'll manage fine on her own, she'll make sure her business doesn't go under. But when she makes that promise Papa Roger and I always know that means she'll go and force the shopkeepers at the Grand Marché to pay back what they owe her. And I bet that to this very day not one of those shopkeepers has settled their debt …

I set the bottle of wine in front of Papa Roger, along with a glass and corkscrew. He's stopped listening to the Voice of the Congolese Revolution, and is now listening to Voice of America, and looking very sad.

'Michel, shots were fired yesterday in Brazzaville …'

I'd like to ask him why they didn't announce that yesterday on the Voice of the Congolese Revolution, why we're being told by Voice of America the next day.

But I don't. If Papa Roger knows the answers to these questions, he'll tell me. That's what he always does if there's something serious on the news, in our country or in the world in general. In any case, we weren't likely to hear, as Brazzaville is over five hundred kilometres from Pointe-Noire, where we are; even if you took the Micheline it would take three whole days. So, for me this story about the firing of shots that hasn't even been reported by our radio station yet could just be some piece of provocation by white and black imperialists, trying to upset our country and the Congolese Socialist Revolution. I want to tell Papa Roger he's wrong to take this news item so seriously, he's heard worse things than that before without getting all upset, and managed to carry on eating his pangolin meat and drinking his red wine and stuffing his nostrils with the tobacco that always makes him sneeze.

I'm not worried; I know our best soldiers are all in Brazzaville. Their job is to train morning, noon and night to intimidate Zaire, i.e. the former Belgian Congo, who long to wage war on us, create chaos in our country and then steal our oil by night, while we're asleep. Also, when you're a really small country like the Congo, if you make loads of noise by firing shots, countries like Zaire piss in their pants and think there are lots of us, that we're hiding in the River Congo and we'll leap out at the crucial moment and attack them, like in the war films they show in our cinemas in Pointe-Noire and Brazzaville.

The Zairian military never train at all, and they still think they're the biggest shots in the whole of Africa. They just sit around in their barracks watching *The Longest Day* and think they'll be able to fight in the water like the Americans. I've already seen *The Longest Day* four or five times at the Rex, it's the only film that's shown right through from Monday to Sunday. As soon as the idiots from the Rex or the Trois-Cents rip down the poster for the film and put it up at home, the cinema owner puts another one up and writes underneath in red pen: *It is forbidden to steal the poster for* The Longest Day. *Fines will be imposed.* They do the same thing on the walls in the rich neighbourhoods, they write, *No litter tipping. Fines will be imposed*, but it doesn't stop people from leaving their manioc leaves or their rotten food in the street, around midnight, when there's no one there to see.

So, these Zairians who want to attack us have got it wrong: the Congo River is different, the Americans can't come to their aid with all their heavy artillery, because there's no beach here, it would be even harder for the Americans because of the dangerous beasts in the water, not to mention Mokélé-Mbembé, the monster that terrifies the Pygmies in the north, even if no one's ever actually seen it …

Papa Roger and I are listening carefully to what they're saying on Voice of America. The names of the American president, Jimmy and Carter, are like names anyone might have, they've got a good ring to them. Jimmy Carter isn't talking about the war that may break out between us and Zaire, he's got something more serious to discuss: he's really angry with that other lot of troublemakers, the Israelis and Palestinians. Instead of getting along nicely they just squabble the whole time, as if they had nothing more important to do. Jessica Cooper, the American journalist, is in a really bad mood too, even worse than Jimmy Carter. She says it just can't go on, we need to give the poor Palestinians a plot of land, or how are they going to feel proud and go round shouting that they exist, if they don't have a country like all the rest of the world?

They've stopped talking about the shooting in Brazzaville now, it was just a flash, and Jessica Cooper says they'll give more information once the journalists they've sent from Kinshasa to Brazzaville know more.

They've stopped talking about arguments between Israelis and Palestinians, they're talking about the St Etienne football team, which Papa Roger supports, and who are top of the French league table. They've lost to Liverpool, who are top of the English league table, and my father is not happy to hear this:

'Anyway, who cares about the English? The Swiss will win in the end; they've got more than enough money to bribe the referees, even the honest ones.'

He takes a couple of swigs of his red wine, and turns the dial on the radio to the Voice of the Congolese Revolution.

'Good God, when are these good-for-nothing Congolese journalists going to tell us what's happening? You'd think they'd have had enough of this Soviet music they've been bombarding us with since yesterday!

The talking tree

That's the third time Maman Pauline's asked us to switch off the radio because it's time to sit down to eat. She says it's not good to eat while you're listening to Soviet music, you won't appreciate the flavour of the food. Also, if you're at table it's better not to know what's going on in the world, that way if you hear bad news it will be too late, you'll already have eaten and belched.

My father and I don't budge, even though Maman Pauline's calling, we stay put under the old mango tree, which is one of our three fruit trees, along with the papaya and the orange tree outside the kitchen. Maman Pauline planted this tree when she bought the land; she likes to tell you how she brought the seed directly from her native village, because the best mango trees in the whole country grow there, and not in Pointe-Noire, where the mangoes look beautiful on the outside but are rotten on the inside. Besides, the mangoes from here are not as sweet as the ones from Louboulou, even the flies know that, they leave them alone.

This tree is a kind of second school for me, and sometimes my father jokingly calls it the 'talking tree'. This is where he always comes to listen to the radio when he gets home from the Victory Palace Hotel. His work is very tiring, so at the weekends he rests here, from morning till sundown, just sitting in his cane chair, with the radio right up close. He could go and lie in his bed and take it easy, but the trouble is, the aerial doesn't really work inside the house, it's like you can hear the sound of popcorn bursting in boiling oil coming from inside the Grundig. Also, it's often just when the news is really important that the voices get all jumbled up and in the end the transistor tells stories that are just not true. A radio should never lie, especially if it was really expensive, and the batteries are still new, because my father sends me to buy them at Nanga Def's, the West African seller with a shop two minutes on foot from Ma Moubobi's.

I'm serious about this thing with a school under the mango tree. For example, this is where my father told me lots of secrets about the war in Biafra, because the Voice of the Congolese Revolution was always talking about it. Our radio informed us that Olusegun Obasanjo, the President of Nigeria, where the war took place, had been congratulated that year by Pope Paul VI for organising a huge meeting of blacks from all over the world. Our journalists, who wanted to be in the good books of the government and Comrade President Marien Ngouabi, started off saying it was a scandal, shouldn't they be congratulating our leader of the Revolution, who'd been working 24/7 to develop our country? They criticised President Olusegen Obasanjo, saying he never wore a collar and tie, he never smiled, he was a disgrace to our continent, and anyway, their war in Biafra was just a war between prostitutes about who was in charge of the streets in Lagos.

'Michel,' my father said, 'don't listen to them! Over two million people have died in two and a half years in this war!'

Papa Roger added that the Nigerians were all killing each other in a real civil war, because some people had decided they were going to create their own separate country, the Biafran

Republic, alongside the normal country, even though this one had been clearly drawn up by the whites in geography books. Again according to Papa Roger, the government of Nigeria was opposed to splitting up the territory because otherwise people would wake up the next day with two enemy countries at war all day long. The government had closed the borders. But if you close the borders with a great big padlock, if people can't come and go as they please any more, how do you get food in? Which is how famine came to Nigeria, with not a single bunch of bananas left to feed people's hunger. Papa Roger had told me quietly – because it was an important secret that he'd heard from the whites at the Victory Palace Hotel – that the French had joined in the war, even though they didn't even colonise Nigeria like they did us. Their president back then, General de Gaulle, had sent a man they called the 'white sorcerer'. This man, whose real name I've now forgotten, was someone who never said very much, and who knows so many secrets about our continent that you wonder who the traitors were who gave him the information and how much he paid them for it. Most black presidents have to talk with the 'white sorcerer' to keep France happy. This is the man who decides who will be the president of the Republic of such and such a country that the French have colonised. And if one of these presidents that the French have put in power criticises the French too loudly at the UN, where they sort out rows between countries that are cross with each other, 'the white sorcerer' gets annoyed and the next day the jumped-up African is no longer president of the Republic, he'll be put in jail, if they haven't already killed him in a coup d'état secretly cooked up in France with other Africans who don't understand they're providing a rod for their own backs and continue to have their riches stolen at midnight when people are in bed dreaming about more important things than oil, which is the cause of so many of our problems.

'So what I'm saying, Michel, is that France has poured a lot of money into this civil war. Both sides in the conflict, the official government and those in favour of dividing the country, asked France for help. And the French chose to support the divisionists and their Biafran Republic. Does that seem right to you?'

Since he'd told me that the French were happy for Nigeria to be split in two, I said to Papa Roger that it was wrong for one country to get involved in another country's fights – if people get into fights and I don't know why they're beating each other up I just walk straight on by and don't look back; I'm only going to fight if I'm provoked or if there's no escape because there's no short cut or the people after me have already caught up with me.

Papa Roger smiled and replied that since the French supported the creation of the Republic of Biafra-next-door, they'd employed mercenaries, who are bandits that get paid to cause turmoil in a country they don't even know. One of these mercenaries – this is a name I *do* remember – was Bob Denard. He's a real specialist in turmoil; before he popped up in the mess in Nigeria he'd been stirring up trouble for the people in Algeria, who were fighting to get their country back from the French. So this Bob Denard's name in French is actually Robert, but Bob sounds scarier for a mercenary. Anyway, Papa Roger didn't like this guy having the name 'Robert' because, he said, the little brother of some American president was also called Robert, although the American Robert had not been making trouble for the people bravely fighting in Algeria to get their country back from the French. When Papa Roger showed me a photo of the American Robert in the newspaper

I was shocked: he was young and handsome. But even though he was young and handsome, the Americans assassinated him when he too could have become president of the United States like his big brother, who'd been shot in a car next to his wife, like in a film.

'Michel, you're dreaming again!'

Papa Roger gives me a shove with his elbow and interrupts me just as I'm sitting happily there under the mango tree with him, thinking my thoughts. He gives a nod and I turn round: Maman Pauline's heading towards us, like an enraged bull.

'Do I have to tell you twenty times to come and eat, instead of sitting around listening to lousy music? Well, you can just eat the radio today! *Bon appétit!*'

I don't want to eat the Grundig or the Soviet music inside it. I want to eat what she's prepared, especially as she announced yesterday that she was going to cook something special for me because she was proud of the good marks I'd got in my second term at middle school.

Papa Roger tries to calm her down.

'We're coming, Pauline, just give us a few more seconds ...'

She zooms back into the house. First we hear the sound of her opening the old cupboard, then of plates smashing on the floor.

'What on earth is your mother doing?' Papa Roger says.

'I think she's punishing the plates instead of punishing us ...'

Mboua Mabé

Maman Pauline comes back towards us. She's carrying a large cooking pot, and her face is even more furious than before, as if we were her enemies in the war in Biafra.

She chucks the whole dish of pork and plantains on the ground, then runs to the front of the plot and shouts:

'Mboua Mabé! Mboua Mabé! Mboua Mabé!'

Mboua Mabé is our dog. He's so thin, you can easily count all his ribs and wonder if he's got another scrap of flesh hiding anywhere else. We bought him three years ago, he was one of those abandoned dogs that people catch in the neighbourhoods and sell at the Grand Marché. Mboua Mabé just kept fixing me with his huge black eyes like he was trying to tell me he was unhappy, and I said to Papa Roger:

'Let's buy that dog, he looks so unhappy ...'

Papa Roger disagreed.

'No, he's a problem dog! He'll do nothing but eat, and he won't even guard the house! Look at him, he's a hypocrite, an enemy of the Congolese Socialist Revolution!'

'He'll guard the house, he won't eat a lot and—'

'Really? How do you make that out?'

'I just feel it, when he looks at me ...'

He burst out laughing; maybe that was when he decided to listen to me.

'I hope you won't regret it!'

I told my father straight away I was going to call him 'Mboua Mabé', which is Lingala for 'bad dog'.

'Honestly! Does a dog need to be told he's a bad dog?'

I thought Mboua Mabé would put on a bit of weight, but in fact he stayed exactly the same, Téké dogs never gain weight.

Mboua Mabé is very polite, he never goes for the bitches that make eyes at him, lying down with their legs spread wide, to get him to do things that I won't go into here or people will say Michel always exaggerates and sometimes he says rude things without meaning to. Whenever I come across a dog in our neighbourhood doing the thing with a female dog, I always feel sorry for them both, two animals stuck together like that, while people throw stones at them, to force them apart, when actually it's just nature taking its course. Mboua Mabé, who is very intelligent, has worked out that if he does the thing with a female dog, he'll find himself stuck to her, while passers-by abuse him with sticks and stones. So the minute he sees a female dog making eyes at him, even if she's very beautiful, Mboua Mabé shakes his head three times to say no, and actually turns his back on her …

So today, Mboua Mabé is the happiest dog in Pointe-Noire, he's got the whole dish of pork and plantains to himself, while I've got nothing, even though I rescued him from the Grand Marché. He's coming forward slowly now. He's pretty suspicious, he's hardly ever had anything but bones, he's not a human, so he doesn't deserve meat.

From a distance he eyes up the meat spilled on the ground, then looks over at my father and me. We signal for him to stay, Papa Roger wags his finger to say no, and I wave my fist to say no as well. Mboua Mabé doesn't know who to obey, he doesn't know if he should be scared of the finger and the fist. So he turns to Maman Pauline, who smiles at him and nods kindly.

'Eat that up for me, Mboua Mabé! Eat it!'

Mboua Mabé drops his ears, wags his tail and heads towards the meal, which Papa Roger and I are eating with our eyes, imagining the pleasure we'd have had.

First he gobbles down the plantains round the edge, saving the big bits of meat for the end. He's excited; his tail's wagging really fast, like a windscreen-wiper. It's a good job Maman Pauline didn't put any chillies in or anything could have happened.

Just as he's tucking into the juicy bit of meat, a violent gust of wind suddenly shakes our mango tree. The birds hidden in its leaves fly off with loud squawks, as though a hunter had taken a shot at them.

I look up: a great big cloud has appeared from nowhere and is blocking out the sun.

The Soviet music has stopped! Yes, it's finally stopped! Papa Roger quickly readjusts the Grundig aerial and we both draw close to the device, which has suddenly gone quiet, though the batteries are still new.

Our heads almost knock, bending over the radio at just the same moment.

I tell myself maybe there is no more Soviet music left for them to play on the Voice of the Congolese Revolution, the radio's used up their entire stock.

The Grundig crackles once, twice, three times. No, it's someone coughing, they're starting to read:

People of the Congo,
A few days ago, during a meeting to mark the celebrations
of the twelfth year of the Revolutionary Union of Congolese

Women, held in the Hôtel de Ville in Brazzaville, the leader of the Revolution, Comrade Marien Ngouabi, announced that sessions of the 3rd extraordinary Congress of our young and dynamic party, the Congolese Party of Labour, would take place shortly. Every Congolese man and woman knows that the 3rd extraordinary Party Congress was about to endow our country with stable revolutionary institutions, to give a fresh boost to our people's struggle for liberation.

Now, with its back to the wall and in its death throes, imperialism has used a suicide unit to launch a cowardly attack on the life of our dynamic leader of the Congolese Revolution, Comrade Marien Ngouabi, who died in combat with his weapon in his hand, this Friday, 18 March 1977 at 14:30 hours.

In the light of the current situation, the Central Committee of the Congolese Party of Labour decided during a meeting today to delegate full powers to a Military Committee of the Party, composed of eleven members whose task will be to prepare a state funeral, to manage state affairs and to assure the protection and security of the people and of the Revolution, until further notice.

The Military Committee of the Party invites the people to stay alert and do whatever is required to protect the Revolution and the national Union, for which President Marien Ngouabi gave his life. A month of national mourning has been declared, starting today.

Victory or death!
All for the people!
Only for the people!

Mboua Mabé stops eating, stares at the radio, pricks up his ears, turns around and dashes out of the plot, barking, while Maman Pauline shouts after him:

'Come back here, Mboua Mabé! Come back, or I swear I'll re-sell you at the Grand Marché!'

He's far away already; we can't even hear him bark …

Chilli in your eyes

There are groups of people everywhere, even outside our house.

People have come out of their homes and are mingling with passers-by – yellow taxis screeching to a halt, Zairian rickshaw boys dumping their produce at the roadside; they're all standing round arguing loudly, as though they could somehow bring Comrade President Marien Ngouabi back to life. It seems to me that the people standing outside our plot are looking for trouble, Papa Roger's going to get annoyed with them because they're stopping him listening to the radio, where they haven't yet explained how our president came to die with his weapon in his hand yesterday, Friday 18 March 1977 at 14:30 hours, as the report just said.

Some go into our neighbours' house to check if all the radios in the neighbourhood reported the same bad news.

Others are weeping, rolling on the ground, clutching the photo of the leader of the Congolese Revolution, shouting that they don't want to live any more, their lives have no point, they want be buried with their Comrade President Marien Ngouabi, they don't know what will become of them, or our country, in the years ahead. They say there will be no electricity, even in the neighbourhoods of the black capitalists; that there'll be shortages of oil, beer and salted fish; that the price of manioc will be higher than pork, pork higher than rents, rents higher than salaries, etc.

I'm meant to cry too; I try, but it's hard. The only way is to rub chilli in my eyes like widows do when they can't squeeze out a tear for their husbands. These widows are just manipulators, putting on an act when actually they're thinking about what they're going to inherit; they know the rest of the family is going to decide on the basis of how many tears they've shed whether they'll get the house or the car, or whether the whole lot will go to the sister-in-law or mother-in-law.

I really want to cry because Comrade President Marien Ngouabi was a good man, and it's sad hearing the Voice of the Congolese Revolution replay the speech he made five days ago for the celebrations of the Revolutionary Union of Congolese Women. When you listen to it, it's as if he's still alive, or knew that he was going to die and is leaving us some profound words, knowing we'd analyse them down to the very last detail after he'd gone.

In this final speech he promised to do whatever he could to prevent us suffering from the economic crisis created by the rich countries, and he added that our people must try to build peace, in spite of the mess made by the imperialists who, after stealing industrial quantities of our wealth, seem to have nothing better to do than hang around and make trouble.

The reason I say that Comrade President Marien Ngouabi definitely knew he was going to leave us for good is because he ended his speech with the words:

When your country is sullied, and has no lasting peace, the only way to wash it and make it whole is with your blood
...

The cranes fly over

If I do use chilli pepper to bring tears to my eyes, like the widows of Pointe-Noire, Maman Pauline's going to get cross with me and probably rub some more in. So to make myself feel sad, I think about the citizenship classes we used to have every week at primary school.

We'd listen to a tape recorder playing the Soviet hymn 'The White Cranes', and we'd have to sing along and though I don't like to boast, I was actually the only one who managed it the whole way through, Russian seems quite a normal language, though of course only a poor shadow compared to French.

There were other Soviet songs too, much the same, with violins, accordion and piano. And the Soviets sing in big deep voices, like us at funerals when we sing like that to compliment the corpse, so at least it feels it was someone important, even though it was actually someone really annoying that no one liked. If you listen carefully, the sadness in the Soviet voices is quite different to the sadness of our singers! We have this false sadness, whereas the Soviets are serious, and sometimes even they forget this isn't just a song for entertainment, and they start weeping for real in their own language. When we put on a sad voice it's actually to explain to the deceased, who's refusing to go and live in the land of the dead, that that's enough now, we haven't an endless supply of tears to carry on weeping for weeks as though he was the unhappiest dead man the country had ever seen. We explain to the corpse it's time to stop acting like he doesn't know any better, like he's completely and utterly without shame before his family. We remind him the neighbours have come round, they've given money, coffee, candles to place around the dead man's bed, white sheets to cover him, they've clubbed together to buy a coffin, so his final voyage passes off smoothly and the other dead people don't make fun of him because his family got into debt to pay for his funeral.

I could sing 'The White Cranes' without any mistakes because my memory helpfully whispered in my ear how many times I'd already been whipped into learning it. The teacher had translated it all into French for us, in case we didn't understand what the Soviets had planted in the words. So every morning after we'd said lots of nice things about Comrade Marien Ngouabi while standing by the national flag in the playground, the minute we got into the classroom, even before we started the fables of Jean de La Fontaine, which we liked because they had intelligent animals in them, animals who could speak French without making any spelling mistakes or grammatical errors, as though they'd been to school too, we recited the first eight lines. I sat in the front row, especially when we'd been warned that some members of the Congolese Party of Labour were coming from Brazzaville to visit the schools in Pointe-Noire. I've still got it in my head:

> *Sometimes it seems to me the soldiers*
> *Who died upon our blood-soaked battlefields*
> *(soaked in blood)*
> *Don't lie in rest, interred in this good earth*

But change into white cranes and fly away ...
And since that time, and to this very day,
They fly above us, moaning as they go
(how they moan)
And is that why we stand in silence here
And wait and watch the sky above?

According to our teacher, those of us about to take the Certificate of Primary Education were the white cranes of the Congolese Socialist Revolution and Comrade President Marien Ngouabi was counting on us to help him develop our country, our continent and the other continents too, including all the European countries who think they're already developed, though they're forever changing presidents and, unfortunately for them, the people vote for the leader, instead of creating a Congolese Party of Labour of their own to teach them how to arrange for their comrade president to stay in power till the day he dies.

When the teacher had finished telling us we were the white cranes of the Congolese Workers' Revolution, he asked a second time, to check if we'd really understood:

'Who are you?'

And we all chanted:

'We are the white cranes of the Congolese Socialist Revolution!'

'And what is your mission as white cranes of the Congolese Socialist Revolution?'

And we all chanted:

'Our mission is to sacrifice our lives for the success of the supreme Mission of Comrade President Marien Ngouabi, for the development of our country, our continent and other continents too, including the countries in Europe who believe

they are already developed, even though they're always changing presidents and, unfortunately for them, the people vote for
the leader, instead of creating a Congolese Party of Labour
of their own to teach them how to arrange for their comrade
president to stay in power till the day he dies.'

And he'd ask the final question, this time louder:

'And who are you?'

And we'd reply, this time louder:

'We are the white cranes of the Congolese Socialist
Revolution!!!'

And we'd jump for joy. We cheered everything, while
despising the poor Europeans and their presidents who
couldn't even stay in power until they died. We were flattered that Comrade President Ngouabi and the people in
the government loved us so dearly, and had given us such an
important mission, unlike the poor pupils in other countries,
whose presidents were not Comrade Marien Ngouabi.

I felt very proud singing 'The White Cranes', even if I wondered how exactly Russian soldiers who'd died in combat
turned themselves into white cranes, who *fly above us,
moaning as they go*, if they weren't sorcerers, like the ones we
have here. Also, you had to actually be there when the white
cranes arrived in Pointe-Noire, otherwise you'd never see one.
All I know is whenever I saw them on the Côte Sauvage I was
disappointed, because although they're called white cranes
they don't have one hundred per cent white feathers, their
feathers are mixed in with black feathers, the black being in
the minority – if they'd been in the majority everyone would
have muddled up the white and the black cranes.

In spite of everything, our lives were happy. Often we were
required to recite the names of the foreign presidents the

leader of our Socialist Congolese Revolution had met. Some only came as far as Brazzaville but others made it to Pointe-Noire, and it was up to us, the white cranes of the Congolese Socialist Revolution, to welcome them. We had to prepare for a whole week, so we'd all seem like nice intelligent children, even if the idiots turned straight back into idiots, which was what usually happened. We were told about the lives of each of these foreign presidents and how they'd been born to be leaders. We had to learn by heart the potted history of their countries, likewise their geography, and sometimes we even had to dress like their people. We'd be wearing coats, gloves, furs and shoes under the midday sun, like Europeans do in the depths of winter, because the sun doesn't always shine over there, which is why lots of countries in that continent went off to colonise hotter places, so they could go there on holiday with their wives, children, sick grandparents, not to mention cats and dogs.

If we weren't dressed up in the costume of foreign countries, we'd go to the airport to welcome the presidents at Pointe-Noire airport dressed just in our school uniform, the girls all in pink and the boys with a khaki shirt and shorts the colour of the sky in the dry season. You had to have your red kerchief round your neck and the badge of the National Pioneer Movement, or the head of the school would cancel the opportunity of a lifetime to see up close the heroes who ruled the entire world and were coming to pick the brains of Comrade President Marien Ngouabi. Some of the names of the presidents were easy to remember, but others were more difficult because they were so complicated that we wondered (privately) how people with such names ever came to be presidents in the first place. But you had to pronounce them correctly and know how to write them out the whole way through. We thought some of the names were written just as they were pronounced or pronounced just as they were written, though we couldn't have been more wrong, so we had to keep practising and putting them into songs to be sung in front of the leaders because if a name's in a song you can't possibly pronounce it wrong, or forget it. Also, there were names that changed all the time, like that of the president of the Popular Republic of China: did you say Mao Zedong, Mao Tsé-toung, Mao Tsé-tung or Mao Tso-tung?

We'd say nice things about the presidents in the hope that they'd give us gifts to take home to show our parents. But when they walked down from their airplanes all they ever gave the schoolchildren was flowers. For this reason the head always put the pretty girls at the front and hid the non-pretty ones behind the really tall boys.

I was at Pointe-Noire airport the day our president greeted Comrade President Nicolae Ceaușescu of Romania. This president had come with his wife, and they were very happy when they heard us singing:

> *Papa Nicolae Ceaușescu has come,*
> *No more hunger*
> *Papa Nicolae Ceaușecsu has come*
> *Eternal light will shine*
> *Maman Elena Ceaușescu is the*
> *Most beautiful woman in the world*
> *Maman Elena Ceaușescu has eyes that are*
> *Brighter than water!*
> *Papa Nicolae Ceaușescu, hurrah!*
> *Maman Elena Ceaușescu, hurrah!*
> *Maman Elena Ceaușescu, hurrah!*

Now what Papa Nicolae Ceauşescu and Maman Elena Ceauşescu didn't know was that when a different president came all we did was change the name and keep the same song. If the next president didn't have his wife with him we just had to sing the president's name on its own at the end.

I was there the day we greeted the president of France. We'd been forbidden to call him 'Comrade President Georges Pompidou', the French Revolution had passed its sell-by date a long time back, and anyway, it wasn't this president who'd started it. We had to call him 'Uncle Pompidou', because according to the teacher and the headmaster he was related to our family, by colonisation, which had been brought to us by his country, and by its language, which we all spoke. Now actually that suited us very well, because we really liked the name Pompidou, it sounded like the name of a good little baby that drinks its bottle and goes to sleep without bothering its parents before seven in the morning. His hair was all combed back, he smiled the whole time, as if he knew us and we were his nieces and nephews. We smiled at him the whole time too, as if we knew him, and he was our real uncle, when in fact he wasn't even black, or Congolese.

I was also there when we sang the name of Comrade Amilcar Cabral, even if he wasn't president of his Republic. They told us he'd helped Guinea Bissau and Cap Vert to become independent countries, when the Portuguese colonisers wouldn't hear of it. Comrade Amilcar Cabral was the one who got the loudest cheers in Pointe-Noire, but unfortunately a year after his visit he was assassinated by Black accomplices and Portuguese imperialists. So he never lived to see independence, which followed in his wake, six months after his death. We were pleased, even so, because thanks to him Guinea Bissau and Cap Vert got independence, like our country. Comrade President Marien Ngouabi loved him, which is why, quite near Brazzaville, there's a school called the Amilcar Cabral Agricultural Lycée. That's where you go if you want to train to be an agricultural engineer, even though people say that there's no point training for that, everyone knows how to do agriculture and how to use a hoe to pick out weeds and plant peanuts, yams and sweet potatoes in the Bouenza region …

After the foreign presidents stopped coming to see us, Comrade President Marien Ngouabi started going to see them. I couldn't tell you if the schoolgirls and schoolboys in the countries he visited apart from Romania and the USSR, Hungary and Bulgaria, sang his name, like we sang the names of their presidents. Once the leader of our revolution returned from his travels, our radio always said he was very pleased, he'd been applauded by millions and millions of people in tears, who didn't want him to leave, but he made his excuses and left because he had not completed his mission, which was to develop our country.

Comrade President Marien Ngouabi had been to see the Ethiopians and greeted their emperor, who was called Haile Selassie I, who Bob Marley sings about in his reggae songs that we listen to in Pointe-Noire. When I saw pictures of the emperor in the newspaper, I asked Papa Roger where the guy got his fine gold medals made – he wears them on his chest, and they're better than the ones the American blacks are given for winning races at the Olympic Games. Papa Roger replied that Haile Selassie I was the King of Kings on this earth. So he was above Comrade President Marien Ngouabi, but they couldn't say that on our radio or the leader of our revolution would be furious. This emperor was so strong and so determined, that even when the whites colonised his country he went on shouting that he was the King of Kings, and refused to recognise white rule.

Our president also met the Comrade President of the People's Republic of China, the one called Mao Zedong, Mao Tsé-toung, Mao Tsé-tung or Mao Tsutung, which isn't surprising, our two countries are brothers, but even so China's the big sister, it was China that funded our hospitals and built the Mouloukoulou dam in Bembé country for us for free, and Papa Roger says it's thanks to the dam that there's electricity all the way to Zaire.

In China schoolgirls and boys turned out to greet Comrade President Marien Ngouabi as this was actually a technique we'd copied from them and the Soviets.

The leader of the Socialist Revolution of the Congo had said something that we had to learn by heart, and which Comrade President Mao Zedong, Mao Tsé-toung, Mao Tsé-tung or Mao Tsötung had liked:

Your people have become a symbol of honour, an example to the entire world of how success can come through hard and honest work. We have come today to drink at the source of this exciting and enriching experiment.

Thanks to these kind words we stopped privately making fun of the name of the Chinese Prime Minister, Chou En-lai. Even so, it did make us laugh, and we'd draw a 'chou' and an 'ail', cabbage and garlic, side by side, and burst out laughing. But since Comrade President Marien Ngouabi had said that it was at the source of this rich and exciting experience that he'd gone to China to drink, we'd left off teasing Chou En-lai, in case he got really cross and went and put poison in said source, which would become like our River Tchinouka, where the poor fish swim about surrounded by a huge army of microbes, gradually dying off before they were lucky enough to be fished and eaten for lunch with foufou, manioc and red pepper.

Comrade President Marien Ngouabi had met our sisters and brothers in North Korea and the president of North Korea, one Comrade Kim Il-Sung, gave him a fine medal because the leader of our revolution agreed with him that they should stop having two countries in Korea, one in the north and one in the south, like when people wanted to divide Nigeria with the Biafra business.

Since our leader of the Congolese Socialist Revolution was already on his travels, he thought he might as well go and say hi to Comrade Leonid Ilich Brezhnev in the USSR, the country where the white cranes flying above people's heads aren't actually real birds, but Soviet soldiers who've died on blood-soaked battlefields. Comrade President Marien Ngouabi felt really at home with the Soviets. A lot of Congolese study over there, and join the Congolese Party of Labour when they come home. Another thing is, it's apparently quite easy to get a Russian woman to marry you, they don't mind if you ask them to marry you, even if you warn them that they're not going to be trafficked, that they'll have to go and fetch water from the river like Congolese women, and eat manioc, foufou or peanut butter with smoked fish with their fingers. They come without a second thought; they can live in our villages and they'll always be happy, as though they didn't really love their own country because of the snow which means you can't see how beautiful they are because their big coats hide the lovely things they've got at the front and at the back, which I won't describe in detail here or people will only say oh that Michel, he always exaggerates, and sometimes he says rude things without meaning to. The Congolese who've been to the USSR say that when Soviet women take off their coats you can immediately see that they're the most beautiful women in Europe, even if, sadly, they don't speak French ...

Comrade President Marien Ngouabi went to see Comrade President Fidel Castro in Cuba, and together they criticised the Americans, who don't want Cuba to develop. Now, the Cubans are our brothers, so they can come to our country whenever they like, including to train our military and help out comrades elsewhere on our continent who are fighting against the accomplices of imperialism. Here in Congo we know the Cubans well, they're in Angola, where their mission is to wage war to protect Comrade President Agostinho Neto against the bad rebel, Jonas Savimbi, who goes round stirring up civil wars everywhere with his accomplices from Portugal, America and South Africa, as if this was still the civil war in Biafra, when anyone who looks at the photo of the two Angolans could tell you straight away that Comrade President Agostinho's the better looking one, and also writes poems we've studied, whereas Jonas Savimbi has never written a poem you'd study in one of our schools. So the Cubans can be expected to give Comrade President Agostinho a bit of a hand. Besides, the Cubans that turn up in Pointe-Noire are really nice to us, drinking beer in our bars, eyeing up the girls' behinds, then dashing off to protect the Angolan president, who is very fond of Comrade President Marien Ngouabi and must be really sad right now ...

The leader of our revolution also visited African presidents. He went to have talks with Comrade President Muammar Gaddafi, hoping they'd get on well together and be able to stop our enemies getting in the way of our development because when we stand firm together imperialism can't find a way in. So he did the same with almost all the African presidents who aim to bring development to our continent and who look after their people properly, as if they were their own children: Siad Barre of Somalia, Gaafar Nimeiry of Sudan, Juvénal Habyarimana of Rwanda, Julius Nyerere of Tanzania, Kenneth Kaunda of Zambia, Macias Nguema of Equatorial Guinea, Jean-Bédel Bokassa of the Central African Republic, Félix Houphouët-Boigny of Ivory Coast, Léopold Sédar Senghor of Senegal, Anwar Sadat of Egypt, Houari Boumédiène of Algeria, Ahmed Sékou Touré of Guinea, Félix Malloum of Chad, Ahmadou Ahidjo of Cameroon, Idi Amin Dada of Uganda, Mobutu Sese Seko Kuku Ngbendu Wa Za Banga of Zaire, Samora Machel of Mozambique, Omar Bongo of Gabon and even the president of Nigeria, Olusegun Obasanjo, who had been congratulated at the start of the year by Pope Paul VI because he'd had the bright idea of organising a huge festival in his country to discuss black culture all over the world.

All this goes to show that Comrade President Marien Ngouabi was not a man to bear grudges; he loved all of Africa just as he loved our country, just as if the people in other countries were Congolese too ...

The runner

Even remembering all the citizenship lessons and the names of the presidents all over the world that Comrade President Marien Ngouabi met with, I still somehow can't get as upset as I should.

I notice a weird guy opposite our house. He's telling off his three boys, I wouldn't like to have a dad who acts like that. I go a bit nearer; I want to hear what he's upset about, why he's yelling at his poor children. He says they mustn't play outside, they must go straight back indoors, tell their mother to close the doors and windows till the funeral for Comrade President Marien Ngouabi is over. He's very small and is wearing wide flared trousers and three-decker Salamander shoes so people will think he's tall, when in fact he's not, it's easy to see he's no giant, when you're a giant you're giant all over: arms, fingers, legs, etc. Comrade President Marien Ngouabi was also very short, and wore those Salamander shoes, maybe that way he thought he wouldn't look small next to the other presidents, like a glass placed next to a bottle of red.

The man's still standing outside our house watching his children move off when he yells:

'Run! Run! Run, for heaven's sake!'

I can see them running towards Voungou Bridge Avenue, as if they were racing, and their dad was timing them all. They don't look back, they just keep on and on running, and the smallest of the three is fastest, like a gazelle.

The three boys keep on running, harder, faster. The little man glances over at our plot and notices me, Michel, standing there by the entrance watching everything like a spy. Our eyes meet. First he's embarrassed, then frightened, and suddenly he starts running too. But he's making for the Tié-Tié neighbourhood, in the complete opposite direction to his boys. That seems really weird, and I think to myself: Could he be going to a different house – to his second or third or fourth wife? I turn round and see my dad wiggling the radio aerial to get a better signal. I can't ask him if the little guy has gone to find his second or third or fourth wife or he'll think I'm just trying to find out if he, Papa Roger, will go off to see Madame Martine, his second wife, who I really like. Madame Martine's children are my brothers and sisters, even though I didn't come out of her belly and I was adopted by Papa Roger before I was even a year old, and Maman Pauline had just arrived in Pointe-Noire after the man who would have been my father, the policeman who made me hate every single policeman in the whole wide world, abandoned us and ran off to Mouyondzi, in the Bouenza region. Papa Roger's always telling me and Maman Pauline that the children he had with Maman Martine are my mother's children too, and my brothers and sisters; that for him there is and never will be any difference between them and me, and when I go and visit Maman Martine in the Joli-Soir neighbourhood she treats me like I've come straight out her own belly and that she knows I love little Maximilien, it's so sweet to see little Félicienne doing her wee-wee on me, and the way Marius chats away to me, and Mbombie respects me and sister Ginette looks out for me, and Georgette, the big sister, is a really good big sister and my big brother Yaya Gaston, who's the big brother to everyone, always wanted Michel – that's me – to live with him in his studio. But I'm lying here now and I always will be. I'm still here, even if I go and see my brothers and sisters sometimes ...

So when I see this little guy running off in the opposite direction to his children, I can't ask my dad:

'Papa, do you have to go to Joli-Soir tonight and tell Maman Martine to shut up the yard and close the doors and windows tight till the funeral of Comrade President Marien Ngouabi is over?'

The Salamanders

They come, they go, arguing, gathering, no one agreeing about how Comrade President Marien Ngouabi came to be dead. And they speak so loud it's as though I was in there with them. There's one who's bald on the sides with a tuft of hair on top who's shouting:

'It's a military plot, everyone knows that! It's not rocket science, the assassins of Comrade Marien Ngouabi are from the Military Committee of the Party!'

A second man, with biceps like Hercules, replies:

'A military plot? It's not a military plot! Don't you know anything about politics? Comrade President Marien Ngouabi did it himself, he was trying to work out how to use his new gun, the one the Soviets gave him last new year for his thirty-eighth birthday!'

'Really? So why did he wait nearly three months to try it? Do people try their guns out at half two in the afternoon? Anyway, Comrade President Marien Ngouabi was at Saint-Cyr, he must have tried out every kind of gun under the sun while he was training there!'

The Herculean guy quickly slaps his hand over his mouth, realising he's said too much in front of the half-bald guy.

'Here we are talking like we know each other. Where are you from, then?'

'Where am I from? You're asking me where I come from? Any reason?'

'No reason, just wondered who I was talking to, and ...'

'I'll tell you where I'm from, I'm from the north, Bangalou- lou, to be exact. But watch out, I've got friends in the south: Laris, Babemes, Vilis, Dondos, Kambas, and more besides; when my father died my own mother married a southerner who was raised by a kindly northerner who—'

'There you go then, you're a northerner! Don't go trying to confuse me; I can see what you're up to! Anyway, why am I talking with a northerner? Now I know why you don't want to hear that the northerners killed Comrade President Marien Ngouabi, even though he was from your region and you're trying to blame us southerners for it! We didn't kill him, you did! It's your corpse, you sort it out, leave us south- erners alone, or there'll be another civil war and the country will split in two, and you can carry on murdering your own brothers to get power, and we'll just look after our oil here in Pointe-Noire all by ourselves, and sell it to the Americans and the Italians and the Spanish, but not to the French – no way!'

'So where are you from?'

'I'm Lari. Is that a problem?'

Our neighbourhood's crawling with military vehicles now.

How come they've got themselves organised so fast? Have the military actually known the news since yesterday? Either way, they move slowly and people first look at them fearfully, then run off like chickens down little side streets or go into the nearest plot, as though the people who lived there were their own family. As soon as the trucks have gone, the chickens all come back out and start peering about them, to see which way the military went. The trucks in question are black, just the hoods are bright red like the Revolutionary flag, and you can't even see the driver and the soldier sitting beside him, because the glass is smoked. You just imagine they can see everything, and if anyone gets up to any mischief they would straight away gun them down.

Papa Roger's really sad, sitting there beside his radio, with his right hand clamped to his cheek, elbows on his knees. Anyone who sees him sitting like that will think Comrade President Marien Ngouabi was a member of our immediate family, maybe even his brother. So, to show him that Michel – that's me – is feeling just as sad as him, wants to be just as sad as him, I go towards him and ask:

'Papa, who do you think will wear Comrade President Marien Ngouabi's Salamander shoes now he's gone?'

The red Renault 5

I thought of nothing else all afternoon. In the end I told Papa Roger I needed to go and look for Mboua Mabé, he'd been gone over four hours.

'Are you serious?'

'I need to find him and—'

'He's only an animal, Michel!'

'But he's my dog, Papa, and besides—'

'The death of the president is more important than the wayward behaviour of a duplicitous and cowardly hound! Were those great bits of pork not enough for him, then? Does he have to go eating from bins all over town into the bargain, so people think we don't feed him properly at home?'

I don't agree.

'It's the radio's fault.'

'How come?'

'If we'd switched it off when Maman Pauline wanted we'd have had a proper meal. Mboua Mabé never eats from the bins in Pointe-Noire, I told him not to ...'

I continue to defend the dog; I tell my dad that just because Mboua Mabé wasn't lucky enough to be born human doesn't mean we shouldn't worry about him. I want to know why he was trembling, why he ran off as if the devil was coming straight out of the Germans' Grundig just to scare him, because he knows who the assassins of Comrade President Marien Ngouabi are. I had promised to protect Mboua Mabé, and he had promised to protect our lot, and us with it. Now if he's gone, the bad men who killed Comrade President Marien Ngouabi will come into our lot and steal first our Grundig then our table, then our chairs, then our stools, then our beds, not to mention the big five thousand franc notes the whites give my father at the Victory Palace Hotel, that are never crumpled, they look like they've been washed and ironed to get them so clean and flat.

Papa Roger listens to me, thinking all the while, with a little smile, while I can't see myself what's so funny about what I've said, it's very serious.

I quickly check my shirt's not on back to front. I do up all the buttons, because it's just begun to feel a bit cooler, with the sun moving over towards the Côte Sauvage, to go and light up lands afar.

I take a step towards the exit of the lot.

I take a second step, then a third, and it's at that moment that Papa Roger grabs me by my shirt:

'No, Michel, you're not going anywhere. It will soon be seven o'clock; the patrols of the National Popular Army are everywhere, making sure people respect the curfew. And the curfew also applies to teenagers like you …

It's not the first time I've heard this weird word 'curfew'. Usually when they talk on the radio about war in Africa, or elsewhere, it crops up at least ten times, along with others like 'ceasefire', 'open fire', 'bloody havoc', 'pools of blood', etc. And it's because of the curfew that we're not allowed to stay out at night till the early hours of the morning. The enemies of the Socialist Revolution hide out among the regular population, then after dark they make all these plans to cause trouble in a country that's never done them the slightest harm. He even tells me the wicked plotters may well come causing trouble here in Pointe-Noire because whenever there's some kind of problem over in Brazzaville, where they talk politics from dawn till dusk, it's always to do with oil.

'And where is our oil to be found, Michel?'

'Here in Pointe-Noire …'

'There you go. Now you get the picture!'

On the other hand I think to myself: Why would they come and stir things up here when it will only be a waste of oil if they start falling over themselves to fight each other like the Nigerians with their war in Biafra, which actually wasn't just a little bust-up with some prostitutes?

'You don't leave this spot, Michel. Mboua Mabé is acting like a local lackey of Imperialism. I never liked that dog! If a mutt refuses real food because someone killed the president you can be sure he's got something on his conscience …'

No, I can't just abandon Mboua Mabé to his fate, all alone in this town of leaderless madmen, because he'll get run over by a car and his body will be left in the street and get eaten by flies, wasps, snakes and other beasts placed on this earth to be a nuisance to us, when they could just go and create their own country.

No, Mboua Mabé is not a mutt. I don't like that word; it makes my dog sound worthless, just like all the other dogs with no master.

No, Mboua Mabé is no hypocrite, whatever Papa Roger thinks. Hypocrites are weird people who hide their intentions and then try to harm you when you're least expecting it. This is Michel telling you, I know exactly what's in that dog's mind, he tells me everything. He always asks me if he can do this, or do that, if he wants to scratch or go and take a rest under the mango tree and he knows if he hasn't got my permission I'll be cross with him.

No, Mboua Mabé does not have rabies. True, he's so thin that even the fleas can't find anywhere to get their teeth into him. But I'm thin too. Does that mean I've got rabies?

Just because Mboua Mabé can't talk back in French or in one of our ethnic languages, we shouldn't go blaming him for everything like he was the scapegoat mentioned by Father Weyler at Saint-Jean-Bosco's, not far from the house of the parents of my friends Paul and Placide Moubembé, who I play football with at the Tata-Louboko stadium. Anyway, Mboua Mabé has proved his intelligence to me by being the only animal in the entire town to be sad, even before I was, when they announced the news of the death of Comrade President Marien Ngouabi on the Voice of the Congolese Revolution. Would any other dog in the world turn their back on a dish of pork with plantains because of something bad they heard on the radio that took place over five hundred kilometres from where he's eating?

Also, I feel less alone with him; he's my brother and my sister too. The reason I'm feeling sad right now, it's not because of Comrade President Marien Ngouabi, it's because of Mboua Mabé. I'm not going to listen to Papa Roger, I'm going to wait till he's thinking of something else then I'll run off and find my dog. For now I just act like I agree with him.

My father still hasn't budged from the mango tree. Now and then he glances over at me – he knows I'm stubborn.

Maman Pauline's making some more food for us, but before she went back into the kitchen she muttered:

'You can thank Comrade President Marien Ngouabi; it's only because he's died you get to fill your bellies today!'

I heard my mother say we were having cod in peanut sauce with manioc and that tomorrow she'd go and buy some real pork meat at the Grand Marché to make the meal we missed today, part of which is now in Mboua Mabé's stomach. But promises like that don't comfort me; I'm not going to get excited about that. I want to find my dog, and I need to leave this house, even if no one's allowed outside after 7 o'clock because of the curfew.

Papa Roger's dozing!

God truly is great, He's one great big God, He's heard my prayer! I can leave the yard now, and go and yell Mboua Mabé's name in the streets, find him and bring him back home again. He's out there somewhere, hiding because he's ashamed, but he just needs to explain to Papa Roger and Maman Pauline and me why he was so naughty. It's also possible, since he never leaves our yard, that Mboua Mabé can't find his way home …

Papa Roger's snoring. That's what happens when he's emptied his bottle of red and had too much tobacco up his nose. I take one step, then two, then a third. I get further and further away.

I'm halfway across the yard now. My heart's beating really fast, I'm afraid my dad will stop snoring and realise I've vanished into the night when there's a curfew.

I can hear a clattering from the kitchen: Maman Pauline's still busy making the dish of cod in peanut sauce; she won't see me leave …

Just as I get to the front gate and try to slip through the barbed wire, because if I push the wooden gate it will creak and everyone will know I'm leaving, a car stops outside our house, its headlights shining right into my eyes.

I put my right hand up to my forehead so I can see what make the car is. It's nothing special, not like the cars of the black capitalists. It's a red Renault 5. I recognise it, I'm sure of it; I've already ridden in it thousands of times, usually sitting next to the driver, which is good, because you can prop up your elbow on the door like some smart guy, so everyone can see.

Yep, I know this red Renault 5: my cousins and I have even sometimes washed it by hand, with Omo.

It's Uncle René's car.

Immediately I turn back into the yard. If my uncle sees me outside, he might say: Michel, where are you off to after curfew?

Two strange men

Uncle René's not alone tonight; he's got two men with him, who I've never set eyes on before. I don't like them already, I don't like the way they're dressed in black suits, as if they'd just come from Mont-Kamba cemetery, or from a family wake in the Chic neighbourhood. Their white ties make me think of them as two lost penguins, frightened of getting separated. One is really tiny and, though I don't like to boast, I'm taller than him even though he's wearing Salamanders with three- or four-storey elevator heels. The other guy looks OK, he's average, his only problem is he's having real trouble getting out of the car, as if his back's been in spasm for years but he's too scared to go to the Congo-Malembé hospital to get treated by the magic Chinese doctors who cure sick people by sticking needles into their bodies.

They're entering the yard now, one behind the other. My uncle's first, followed by the average-size man with the stoop, and then the little fellow with a black briefcase in his hand. I recognise that briefcase: it's Uncle René's. I always admired the way my uncle opened it at his house by pressing on a button, taking out really important papers, correcting lots of things with his red Biro like our French teacher at the Three-Glorious-Days, even though he sells cars in the town centre and talking's more important than writing for selling cars.

Papa Roger is standing to attention before them. This is mostly out of respect for Uncle René, who, by becoming too rich, is now a black capitalist, the only one in our family, even though his car, which he changes three or four times a year, is no nicer than the ones driven by the black capitalists I meet when I go to buy things at Case by Case or from Nanga Dèf, the Senegalese.

No, Maman Pauline isn't standing to attention like my father, she's on her knees in the middle of our yard. Anyone watching this scene would find my mother ridiculous, in this praying position, but among our people, the Babembe, it's what younger sisters or brothers do to show respect to their big sisters or brothers.

The three visitors all want to be the one to help my mother to her feet. Her tears are running right down her neck. Does she suspect that the news they're going to give us is worse even than the death of Comrade President Marien Ngouabi, or Mboua Mabé's disappearance?

She's back on her feet. She brushes the dust off her by flapping a bit of cloth about her knees and anywhere else where they show her there's still some left. Then they all embrace, talking in Bembé. Uncle René's Bembé is easy to understand: he mixes up so much French with it that you'd think French was copying words from our language, when in fact it's the other way round.

I'm standing behind them. Maman Pauline turns around, points at me and says to the two strangers:

'This is Michel ... Your nephew ...'

The man who is afraid of the Chinese doctors at the Congo-Malembé hospital is amazed:

'What? This strapping young man is Michel? No! It's not true, Pauline! How he's grown! The boy's going to be taller than General de Gaulle! When I think how I held him in my lap and he messed all over me! I guess I could have made an effort to see him more often, but with my responsibilities ...'

The little man carrying my uncle's briefcase takes two steps back and takes stock of me:

'Well I never! How very rude! He's bigger than I am! What do they feed you on, I wonder! My oh my!'

Uncle René is dressed all in white. He has a shiny badge on the left lapel of his jacket, which he's worn ever since he joined the Congolese Party of Labour. He dresses in white so that even now with the curfew, even at a distance, people will notice his round red badge that reminds me of Father Weyler's biscuits at the church of Saint-Jean-Bosco during catechism, when I was still in reception class. Back then Father Weyler would warn us, brandishing a whip above our heads:

'Only one holy wafer each, children!'

Now, the wafers were so sweet that the more you ate the more you wanted. So we'd do three rounds, slipping behind the priest, who wore heavy glasses and never noticed he was giving a wafer to the same child three times over.

Uncle René's badge shows two green palms, one on the left, one on the right. Above the palms, as on our country's flag, is a yellow star and underneath, also in yellow, are a hammer and a hoe, crossed in an 'X'. If people see this badge, even on a second-hand shirt, they tremble; they're afraid because they think it means you're known to members of the government and you'll end up as a minister one day. Also, with this badge, you can travel for free on the Micheline, in first class, with air conditioning, and in town, if your car gets stuck in mud because of heavy rain, people will give you a push. And that's not all – if you shop at the Grand Marché, you'll have several people arguing over who'll carry your shopping to your car, even if you don't give them any money for it ...

In fact, I'm a bit worried about this little man, with his mouth like a suction cup. As Maman Pauline has made us another meal, after the one we lost, he's bound to stuff himself silly, like someone with no manners. I know what my mother's like; she'll keep serving him over and over till there's nothing left in the pot. I can just see those pieces of manioc disappearing into his mouth four or five at a time, then hurtling down four or five at a time into his stomach, which is no small distance, as the little man in question has the biggest belly I ever saw. Perhaps I'm getting too worked up, and he actually ate before coming here, because his belly is all swollen. Perhaps the death of Comrade President Marien Ngouabi will have made him lose his appetite, though not the disappearance of Mboua Mabé, or maybe the real greedy guts is the man who's afraid of the Chinese doctors at the Congo-Malembé hospital who'll turn into a normal man once the food's been put on the table. Anything's possible, so I'm going to keep a careful watch on both of them, even if in *The Lion and the Gnat* by Jean de La Fontaine we're told that the enemies most to be feared are the little ones ...

Maman Pauline asks me to bring out the chairs and put them under the mango tree.

Uncle René disagrees:

'Pauline, we have important things to talk about. We can't do it outside, you'll see why ...'

I don't let on that I'm quite happy to stay outside while they discuss their secret, which has nothing to do with me, and can't be discussed outside. While they're doing that, Michel – that's me – will sneak off and look for Mboua Mabé.

They go inside the house, Papa Roger last, carrying the Grundig. I go back to the foot of the tree. I sit on the basketwork chair as though I'd actually turned into Papa Roger. I think about how the curfew's intimidated people because if they hang around out of doors the police will accuse them of having plotted against Comrade President Marien Ngouabi. It's like in a different Jean de la Fontaine poem we had to recite, 'The Hare's Ears', where an animal with horns has wounded the lion and the lion gets really angry with all animals with horns. When the hare sees the shadow of his own long ears he thinks the lion might think he's got horns too, and that the king of the animals might eat him up without listening to what he has to say! It's the same with the curfew: when you're outside you looked like an animal with horns, and the lions will eat you without listening to what you have to say. So, when I'm in the street later, if I'm unlucky enough to see a truck full of soldiers, all sad and angry because of the death of Comrade President Marien Ngouabi, I'll go and hide either behind a tree or in one of those deserted houses where the madmen of Voungou live. Michel – that's me – knows the neighbourhood better than the soldiers. For example, I know how to get to the Avenue of Independence by going through the neighbours' yards, but the soldiers will have to ask for directions and if no one tells them right they'll carry straight on and end up in the River Tchinouka, where the poor fish swim around in bacteria and die before they get the chance to be fished out and eaten at midday with foufou, manioc and red pepper. On the other hand, who are the soldiers going to ask for directions when they're lost because they said on the radio that everyone has to stay in their houses? They're not exactly going to go knocking on every door saying, ''Scuse me, we are brave soldiers from the National People's Army, we're looking for the murderers

of Comrade President Marien Ngouabi and we want to get to
Mbota without going via Voungou, where there's too much
witchcraft, but we're lost, can you help us please?' At military school our soldiers don't learn that you're not allowed to
joke in the Voungou neighbourhood, which, as I've already
said, used to be a Vili cemetery, that's the southern tribe that
eats sharks, as if there weren't plenty of other smaller fish in
the sea. So the devils and ghosts that still live below ground
don't care about the curfew because everyone knows they only
go out at night because if they go out in the day the light's
going to hurt their eyes, they won't be able to be scary any
more, so what would the point be then of being devils and
ghosts? So, as soon as the spirits hear the sound of big military trucks driving about there'll be total chaos and mayhem
underground, they'll all come out and no one will know who's
human and who's a ghost, and who's a devil, because some
of the devils and some of the ghosts will be wearing military
uniform so they can mingle with the trucks carrying soldiers
of the National People's Army!

But I don't need to worry about that. If the soldiers bump
into me are they really going to think I'm part of a plot, when
in fact I'm alone and, if you think about it carefully, you need
at least two people, one person on their own can't plot with
themselves! So they'll say to themselves: 'Listen, lads, let him
go through, he hasn't got a beard yet, not like those Lari rebels
being hunted and bombed down in the Pool region. He's just a
poor young boy who maybe hasn't eaten yet and is on his way
home; people his age don't kill the president of the Republic, not in this country.' And they'll snicker while I go on my
way, looking for Mboua Mabé. But then if their leader, who
wants to prove to the other military that he's in charge of
making sure people respect the curfew rules, insists that they

take me to be whipped with the drive chain of a Motobécane
AV42 moped, well then I'll have to explain to this leader that
Michel – that's me – is looking for Mboua Mabé, who's run
away from home because he felt really sick when he heard the
terrible news on the radio, while other dogs are loafing around
at home, especially the dogs that belong to black capitalists
who don't care about the death of Comrade President Marien
Ngouabi, those are the dogs who need whipping with a Motobécane AV42 drive chain. And if my explanation doesn't work
I'll just find another one that the leader of the military will
have no choice but to accept otherwise he'll have problems
with the leaders above him: I will tell him that Michel – that's
me – loves Comrade President Marien Ngouabi as I love Papa
Roger, that I became a white crane of the Congolese Revolution in primary school, that our comrade president relied on
my comrades and me because it was thanks to us he was going
to be able to develop this country, this continent and other
continents as well, including the countries of Europe, even if
they're developed already, they change presidents too often
over there and unfortunately it's their people who choose their
presidents, instead of leaving that difficult and complicated
task to the brave militia, or to their own Congolese Party of
Labour ...

I raise my right leg to slip through the barbed wire without
hurting myself, but just as I'm about to do the same thing
with my left leg and step out into the street, I hear Uncle René
inside the house, shouting: 'Michel! Michel! Michel! Where've
you got to?'

I want to keep quiet, but if I do that my uncle might get
annoyed and think I've been badly brought up. I wait for a
moment then for a moment more. If he doesn't hear me he'll

think I've gone. That will be even worse, because they'll set out to look for me, while I'm trying to look for Mboua Mabé. Now it's difficult to go looking for someone who's also looking for someone else, especially if the someone else is an animal who can get through places a human being can't. The result being that no one ever finds anyone.

I don't want my family to worry. I don't want Uncle René to get really cross with me and say I can't visit his fine, solidly built house in the Comapon neighbourhood, where I've sometimes admired his black briefcase, the one he opens at the press of a button to take out extremely important papers and correct them with a red Biro, like our French teacher at the Three-Glorious-Days, when in fact he just sells cars in the centre of town and to sell cars you need to be able to talk rather than write.

I come back inside our plot and now I'm back in the house again. Everyone's looking at me in silence, as though it was my fault someone had just killed Comrade President Marien Ngouabi.

Is there any more manioc left?

Maman Pauline's put an old cloth with holes in on the table; she only does that for really important guests. It's got old wine stains on it that won't wash out, even though my mother cleans it with hot water and Monganga soap, which is made in Pointe-Noire and is better than soap from Marseilles, which everyone in this town adores. Monganga soap from Pointe-Noire is stronger than *savon de Marseille* because as well as washing your plates clean it can also cure mange.

Maman Pauline has a good technique for hiding the wine stains and holes in the cloth: she covers them with plates. If someone moves their plate, she puts it back where it was as fast as a chameleon catching a fly with its tongue, and smiles at the guest, while Papa Roger pulls a long face because whenever he tells my mother he's going to buy a new cloth she says:

'Why? What's the problem? My own mother, Henriette Nsoko, used this cloth back in Louboulou, do you not want it in your house?'

The glasses on our table don't match, but they are very pretty because they were given to my father by the boss of the Victory Palace Hotel.

'What were you getting up to outside, Michel?' Uncle René asks me. 'I want you to stay indoors with us! Sit down, I'm going to introduce you to two uncles you don't know ...'

Uncle René sits facing Papa Roger and the two men. As I step forward to sit down next to my father and the two strangers, Uncle René blocks my path:

'No, Michel, come and sit here next to me ...'

I like this; all of a sudden I'm more important than the two men. I sit beside my uncle and I can already smell his nice perfume. He's the only person who has perfume like this, the ones I smell in the street are rubbish; they smell like *Mananas*, which they use on dead bodies so they won't smell bad when they arrive in the land of the dead.

I'm admiring Uncle René's badge, which lets him go out even after curfew. One day I'll have one too, I'll be a member of the Congolese Party of Labour, I'll wear a white suit and hold meetings with weird men like the two here this evening.

Papa Roger gives me a look. He doesn't like me being impressed by my uncle. But Uncle René is, after all, my mother's brother, they both came out of the belly of the late Henriette Nsoko, who's dead now, and who Maman Pauline wept for for a whole month in this house after the corpse had been buried back in the village, where she went with Uncle

René. Uncle Mompéro went too, he actually made the coffin, which was so beautiful that the other people buried that day all got the sulks.

'Michel,' my uncle continues, 'allow me to present your uncle Jean-Pierre Kinana, he's got a few back problems, he had a car accident when he was young, on his way to the careers guidance and grants centre to pick up the original of his Baccalaureate diploma and plan his trip abroad, where he was to continue his studies. He was hit by a bus near the Revolution roundabout, and spent nearly two months in the general hospital in Brazzaville. To me Jean-Pierre is a great example of courage, because he got back on his feet, took his destiny in his own hands and continued his studies. During his convalescence, since he wasn't able to travel, he did a second Baccalaureate, with good marks, and went off to study economics at the Lumumba University in Moscow! Today Jean-Pierre is advisor to the Minister for Rural Economy.'

He stops for a few seconds, looks at Maman Pauline, then at me.

'You see, Michel, perseverance pays sooner or later! I have a great deal of time for Jean-Pierre. And another thing is, from primary school through to university, he never had to repeat a year! And he finished top of his year in the USSR! You could go a long way in life too, if you concentrated instead of day-dreaming all the time ...'

Uncle Jean-Pierre Kinana's bobbing his head about like a lizard. Does that mean he agrees with Uncle René saying I look like a 'daydreamer', or is he flattered to have it mentioned that he never repeated a single year, from primary school through to university?

If he knew what I know about the USSR, he'd calm down a bit and not put on that face, as if he's got a lot to be proud of. He doesn't know Papa Roger has told me that studies in the USSR are really easy, because Africans who go there never have to repeat a year; the Soviets want lots of people to be able to speak their language, especially Africans. So they're all very nice to us, and we come home with a big fat diploma, when in fact real diplomas are really small and hard to get, like in fishing, where it's easy to catch a big fish, but you have to struggle a thousand times harder to catch a little one that tastes better. Does Uncle René mean that I should go and do really easy studies later on at the Lumumba University in the USSR so I can come top of my year like this uncle?

When I heard Uncle René say the name Lumumba I looked across at my father, and he winked at me, which meant yes, that was the same Patrice Lumumba he told me about one day under the mango tree, along with all the mayhem that went on back when Zaire was still called the Belgian Congo. He'd talked to me about this hero because I'd asked him why there were primary schools, colleges and lycées all over the place named after Patrice Lumumba instead of the current president of Zaire, Mobutu Sese Seko Kuku Ngbendu Wa Za Banga, which actually means 'Mobutu, the warrior who goes unstoppably from victory to victory'. True, the name is a bit long for a school, a college or a lycée, you couldn't possibly find enough room on a sign to write it all on one line and also draw in the face of Mobutu Sese Seko Kuku Ngbendu Wa Za Banga, with his big glasses and his leopard-skin hat. Papa Roger revealed to me that the Zairian president had plotted with the Americans and the Belgians to kill Patrice Lumumba. A Belgian militiaman dragged him up to a tree, another gave the order to four Africans from the Belgian Congo to take aim and shoot at Lumumba and his two friends, all in the presence of the soldiers and black ministers from the Belgian Congo who were all watching as if it was a show put on for their entertainment, with actors to be applauded by them at the end. After that the Belgians said the three bodies had to be got rid of quickly, or there would be problems, because Africa and the whole of the rest of the world knew that Lumumba had fought for the Belgian Congo to become independent. So they got out their knives – Chop! Chop! – and carved the bodies up into pieces of meat and threw them in a drum of acid to dissolve them. Which is why, to this day, no one knows exactly where the bodies of Lumumba and his friends are. I said to Papa Roger that I didn't understand why they accused President Mobutu Sese Seko Kuku Ngbendu Wa Za Banga of having been involved in this butchery, when he wasn't the butcher. My father was pleased with this remark, and had expected it, and he began to unfold the history of Zaire, which is more complicated than a spider's web.

'Michel, when the Belgian Congo became independent in June 1960, Joseph Kasa-Vubu was made president of the Republic and Lumumba was made prime minister, which was now free and no longer run by the Belgians. You can't imagine what that moment meant to us. Even in our country, which was still called the French Congo, we danced the rumba to "Independence Cha Cha", which Grand Kallé, one of their great musicians, sang to celebrate this tremendous victory. But misery always hides behind the door marked "joy": a few months after independence, the man who then still went by the name of Joseph Désiré Mobutu, a journalist, head of general staff and a member of Lumumba's government, took power by force! No one understood what was going on because Lumumba and Mobutu were thought to be friends. Alas, with the connivance of the Belgian ambassador, this Mobutu first put Patrice Lumumba under house arrest in Kinshasa, then transferred him to the Katanga region. They put him there, where he was hated by the cronies of Moïse Tshombe, President of the State of Katanga, a territory of the Belgian Congo with separatist tendencies, so he could be eliminated without trace and—'

At this point I interrupted my father, even though he hates that and always asks me to let him finish his sentence:

'Why didn't they kill him in Kinshasa?'

'Why not indeed? The problem was that everyone who loved him in Kinshasa had taken up arms to free him! It was chaos, even the other prisoners were angry and backing the hero of independence. They wanted to free Lumumba, put him back in power in place of Mobutu. So killing him in Kinshasa meant risking a whole heap of trouble. By transferring him to Katanga State, where they hated him because his men were giving the regime down there a hard time, they were as good as sending him to his grave, and they let suspicion hover over Moïse Tshombe ...'

After Papa Roger had explained all this I began to really like Lumumba. He didn't want the two Congos to be split into two countries; that was a decision taken for us by the whites and their black accomplices. If they'd asked us what we really felt about it, we'd have spoken up and said that we wanted to stay one single country, one single people, with a single comrade president of the Republic and no plots from the Belgians, the Americans, and their African accomplices who were only too keen to murder black heroes and dissolve their bodies in acid.

'What's going on in your head, Michel? Were you daydreaming again, while I was talking?'

Uncle René's just given me a shove with his elbow. Now he goes on with his introductions:

'The man sitting next to your uncle Jean-Pierre Kinana is your uncle too, his name's Martin Moubéri. His mother is the ninth wife of my father Grégoire Massengo, your maternal grandfather. Martin Moubéri is the chief of staff of the National Social Savings Bank, based in Brazzaville. He is the younger brother of Luc Kimbouala-Nkaya, your other uncle, who's a captain in the National Popular Army in Brazzaville.'

I pretend to be pleased: I nod my head all the way through these explanations. Uncle Martin Moubéri stares right into my eyes, to see if I'm impressed. I ask him:

'So what, exactly, does the chief of staff of the National Social Savings Bank do?'

He rubs his hands together and pulls his tie tighter, so he's looking good.

'Very good question, nephew! But I wouldn't wish to monopolise the conversation with panegyrics to my most modest self here in the presence of elders as illustrious as René and Jean-Pierre not to mention brother-in-law Roger ...'

Uncle Kinana presses him to speak:

'Go on, Martin, you are a model for all our family, I've often told you: your modesty will be the death of you!'

'All right then, if you insist, I've got no choice! Well, I'll be brief ...'

He leans over to me.

'Well, Michel, I hire, fire and sort out personnel problems.'

'Is that all?'

'What do you mean, is that all?'

'Well, to hire or fire people, Papa Roger told me you just send a letter and—'

'Do you have any idea what you're saying, nephew? Really, children these days! How rude!'

Uncle Kinana calms him down:

'It doesn't matter, Martin ...'

Uncle Moubéri pushes his face towards me again.

'You think it's easy, do you, a job like mine? Well, not just anyone can do it! My profession's not easy, my boy! Everything is political, and every decision I take has to be perfectly thought through, I might say *beyond* perfect. Every time I fire someone, I get a phone call the next day from a minister who won't say clearly what he wants, but who asks me very quietly how long I've been working in the public sector, he pretends to congratulate me and asks me to say hello to someone who works under me. Now, do you know who it is I'm supposed to say hello to? I'll tell you, it's his nephew! And it's the same guy I fired yesterday. So what do I do? I get the person I fired back in my office again, and I apologise, and explain that I made a mistake and that his uncle, the minister, says to say hello! It's not at all straightforward, my boy ... What I mean is that my job is strategic, and to keep it you have to be strategic too. My strategy is to be a snail: I give the impression I'm floundering in my own slime, but somehow I manage to make progress ... Anyway, I'm getting worked up, I apologise ... Let me try to explain another way ... I'm actually one of the most respected people at the National Social Savings Bank. People feel intimidated when they arrive at my office, maybe because of the red carpet I personally chose and had fitted. The walls are painted sky blue – which relaxes me because it's not an easy job hiring the right people to the right job, or being the one who has to tell women and men with children that they're no longer on board. In both those cases, the head of personnel isn't going to be popular. In the first case people will say he should have hired such and such a person, who was better; in the second they'll bear a grudge against him for firing so-and-so who's got six wives, twenty-four children to feed and school, funeral costs to pay, a mortgage to pay off, and all the rest …'

I'm only half listening because I can tell now this uncle's just a boaster.

Maman Pauline's already left the table.

When did she disappear? Probably when my thoughts were somewhere away with my hero, Patrice Lumumba.

Maybe she's outside, or in the kitchen. Or perhaps instead of sending me on an errand she's gone to buy drinks from our neighbours at the back, the Boko Songos, who have an emergency drinks stand. If she'd asked me to go, I'd have jumped at the chance to go and look for Mboua Mabé.

The Boko Songos don't have a real drinks stand, it's just a cooler in their living room and people go there when they've run out and don't want to walk all the way to Case by Case. Every time I go over there, Monsieur Boko Songo teases me because once, from our tree, I was spying on what was going on in their plot. But it was a long time ago, when I was only six or seven. Papa Roger had forbidden me to climb the tree; he knew I was peeping at Pélagie, the only girl of the three Boko Songo children, when she went to the toilet, which, like ours, has no roof, so it's easy to see what people look like without their clothes on. One day Pélagie realised what I was up to, because she looked up when a mango fell as I swapped branches to get a better look, because the leaves were in the way. She cried out, as though she'd been stung by a bee, then she quietly went and told her father, and he went straight to tell Maman Pauline and she went straight to tell Papa Roger. It ended badly for me, because I got no dinner that evening, though my father did secretly give me a big piece of meat and some manioc, which I ate under the bedclothes …

My mother comes back into the room with two bottles of wine and a grapefruit juice. This all comes from the Boko Songos', I know that, because I can see the pips floating in my drink, and it's always like that at their stand, they want to show their grapefruit juice isn't like the ones out of a tin or bottle, that they make it themselves.

Maman Pauline passes behind Uncle René, she puts the plates down in the right places, to hide the holes and wine stains on the cloth. It's almost time to eat, and I haven't forgotten I need to keep a close eye on Uncle Moubéri's suction-cup mouth.

'Pauline, don't trouble yourself; we've already eaten, we haven't come for that,' Uncle René says.

I'm thrilled to hear this, but I stay calm and try to look really disappointed that the two uncles and especially Uncle Martin Moubéri won't be eating with us.

Maman Pauline's upset.

'I'm sorry, René, but you are going to eat here! And where did you eat already, if I may ask?'

Uncle René looks at each of the uncles in turn.

'Your two brothers arrived in a plane that took off from Brazzaville four hours ago. Luckily your brother Jean-Pierre Kinana can twist a few arms, or they'd never have got two places, because since yesterday everyone's been trying to get out of the capital. So as soon as I picked them up at the airport we went to get something to eat ...'

Uncle Martin Moubéri confirms this:

'Oh yes, sister, and René certainly did us proud, at the Atlantic Palace Hotel! We had caviar and salmon, not to mention rounding it all off with a whole turkey!'

Uncle René gives him an angry look, almost as though the uncle had been about to reveal something that was meant to stay a secret between the three of them, because in our house we don't eat caviar or salmon, that's food for whites and black capitalists who don't realise that a dish of pork with plantains is a thousand times more delicious and gives you better burps than fish, which just makes you hungry two hours later because it's only tickled your palate.

Uncle Moubéri, as I've said, is obviously a boaster, because we've heard about the red carpet and the sky-blue walls in his office, and now it's caviar and salmon followed by a whole turkey, as though turkey was for dessert.

He strokes his big belly, the kind you get if you eat too much salmon and caviar.

'Sister, I'm telling you, there's no room left here ...'

'Well, you'll just have to find some room, Moubéri! Are you telling me I made all this for nothing?'

Uncle Jean-Pierre Kinana makes signs to Uncle Moubéri to shut up, and he quickly changes his tune:

'Very well, sister, if you really insist, I'll make an effort, but I'll only have two or three spoonfuls. A little bit of manioc and pepper, that's all, I really couldn't ...'

I'm still watching these two Brazzaville uncles carefully, and I understand now why they're wearing jackets that make them look like lost penguins: because people who travel by plane have to be clean, or they'll dirty the seats. I envy them, because I don't know how things work up there, and whether once you've taken your seat you can open the window and watch the cranes flying alongside, trying to find a place where it's warm. And I think to myself, The plane must be really fast, because Comrade President Marien Ngouabi was killed yesterday and these two uncles are in Pointe-Noire today already, whereas if they'd taken the Micheline they'd have arrived the day after tomorrow because of the derailments and the drivers with a girl in each station who have to stop all the time and have a bite to eat and lots of other things besides, which I won't go into here or people will say that Michel, he's always exaggerating and says rude things without meaning to. It's still pretty magic, because if I've got this right, they got the plane today and they also arrived today, then Uncle René went to pick them up and they went to the restaurant at the Atlantic Palace Hotel and ordered salmon, caviar and a whole turkey for dessert, all in under four hours. Flying really is flying!

Maman Pauline brings back a huge dish and puts it on the table. There's cod in it, with peanut sauce, it smells really good. She brings another dish, this one with pieces of manioc in. The pepper's so red, so gorgeous, if you're not careful you'll just wolf it down before mixing it in with the fish and manioc.

Uncle René helps himself first, then Uncle Jean-Pierre Kinana, then Uncle Martin Moubéri, who just takes two spoonfuls, like he promised, with a piece of manioc and one red pepper.

My mother says she's not hungry, when you make the food the smell's so strong, you don't want to eat it; you've already eaten it all up with your eyes.

It's Papa Roger's turn to help himself now, no problem there, he fills his plate up, his belly's not forgotten that we had nothing to eat at lunchtime, as Mboua Mabé ate most of it.

I help myself like Papa Roger, I get straight to it: in goes the first mouthful. It's so good, I close my eyes. My whole body's trembling, it's worried there won't be enough food for my heart, my liver, my pancreas, my small intestine and all the other bits they taught us at primary school in natural science lessons. I tell myself to calm down, no need to worry, Uncle René and the two other uncles ate their caviar, their salmon and their one whole turkey for afters at the Atlantic Palace Hotel. They won't eat much, they're only trying to please Maman Pauline, but their stomachs don't like the idea of going straight from black capitalists' food to food for the people.

My mother's right next to me. I'm in between her and Uncle René, who's only eating half as much as I have on my plate.

Uncle Kinana's also only taken a tiny portion, and as for Uncle Martin Moubéri, he's hardly got more than a baby's dribble, but all of a sudden he chucks the whole lot into his great big suction cup. There goes his jaw, chewing, chewing, chewing. He closes his eyes, like he's just realised this food is better than the caviar and the salmon and the one whole turkey at the Atlantic Palace Hotel. So he takes two more spoonfuls, then three more, then four after that. He spears a piece of manioc and it's gone – just like magic! After a moment or two I realise both the uncles have helped themselves several times over, and there's no more manioc in the big dish. Uncle Martin Moubéri, who didn't want to eat to start with, asks my mother:

'Say, Pauline, is there any more manioc left?'

The polygamous priest

We've been eating for nearly an hour. Uncle René gets more and more antsy as the minutes pass. I can see he wants to say something really important, and is worried he'll put us off our food. No one's speaking, so you can hear the sound of forks, of spoons scraping on dishes, of Uncle Moubéri's suckermouth going, Slap! Slap! Slap!

I don't know what comes over me all of a sudden, but I ask my uncle:

'Uncle, was it the northerners or the southerners that murdered Comrade President Marien Ngouabi?'

Maman Pauline pinches my leg really hard under the table. Uncle René sees her and says:

'Pauline, he's bound to ask questions like this. Everyone in the country's wondering the same thing right now ...'

He sits up straight, touches his Congolese Party of Labour badge, raises his wine glass and wets his lips slightly before setting it down again:

'Things aren't quite that straightforward, Michel ... Why do you think the northerners might have killed our president?'

'Maman said so, when we heard the news on the radio.'

Everyone turns towards Maman Pauline as I continue:

'And she said the northerners, especially the Mbochis, aren't usually as clever as us, they're not normal, they're bad people, and from the moment they're born their parents tell them they have to be soldiers and go and kill southerners and presidents of the Republic who aren't northerners. And also, I—'

Maman Pauline kicks me under the table. Again, Uncle René sees her and says:

'Anyway, what does "normal" mean, Michel? I'm sure Maman Pauline didn't mean what you think. I know my sister, she's not a woman to harbour hate. Besides, she's the only one in our family who speaks a northern language – Mbochi! And let me tell you, it's not easy ...'

He goes on flattering Maman Pauline, who has folded her arms to show us how cross she is that I've betrayed her.

'We've seen everything in this country, Michel ...'

So now he starts talking about the old days, when the French colonised us, then how the French decided that our first prime minister would be a polygamous priest, Fulbert Youlou, a Lari, so a southerner. In the 1950s we didn't have a president of the Republic; the polygamous priest was just prime minister. Uncle René goes on to explain how, tangentially, the northerner Jacques Opangault got thrown out. His title was 'Vice-president of the Governmental Council', appointed by the French, who were therefore replacing a northerner with a southerner, which was how many people saw it, especially the northerners. The polygamous priest started to live the high life, like he'd stopped being a representative of God, even his cassocks were made by top designers in Europe. His four wives were all official, but everyone said he had mistresses left, right and centre. Uncle René added that the polygamous priest had imprisoned the northerner Jacques Opangault, then released him a few months later, and that he'd granted himself powers that allowed him to change our Constitution and throw out members of our National Assembly and get himself elected first president of our country in 1959 ...

As I listen I start to think that maybe this is how Uncle René talks every Sunday to the new members of the Congolese Party of Labour at the Party School in the Mouyondzi neighbourhood. While some people go to church, Uncle René goes to this old building, which used to be a soap factory, and teaches newcomers how to be members of the Party and understand the history of our country. The schoolchildren in Pointe-Noire have to go and visit the Party School with their teachers, it's part of the citizenship course. Inside the walls are covered with black-and-white photos of Lenin, Karl Marx, Engels, Mao Tse-tung, Stalin, Fidel Castro, Leonid Brezhnev, Tito and comrade Nicolae Ceaușescu. But the best photo of all is the one of Comrade President Marien Ngouabi in his para-commando uniform, with people all around him, congratulating him on having jumped out of a military plane without breaking his legs.

'Michel, you're dreaming, everyone else is listening to me ...'

I sit up straight. It's true, everyone's looking at me, and Uncle René carries on, calmly:

'The polygamous priest gradually got more and more bourgeois, he developed a taste for luxury, fine houses, built up his personal fortune while the Congolese people ate caterpillars and earthworms! When there were strikes he imprisoned the trade unionists, like during the three days of the thirteenth, fourteenth and fifteenth of August, nineteen sixty-three – our 'Three Glorious Days', as they're called – when he countered demonstrations with imprisonment, but then people went to the detention centre to free the poor prisoners. After that the polygamous priest was finished, they'd had enough of him and his government. He had to flee, and died in exile in Europe …'

Uncle Jean-Pierre Kinana gives a little cough. Now it's his turn.

'Brother René, with respect, we should remember it was under the regime of Alphonse Massamba-Débat, who replaced the polygamous priest, that we started to have political assassinations in this country. Remember the Public Prosecutor, Lazare Matsocota – he was a cousin of the polygamous priest!'

'Exactly, Jean-Pierre! Why did they kill him? Because when President Massamba-Débat offered him the post of Minister for Justice he turned it down? Or because people thought of him as the natural successor to his uncle, the polygamous priest? I knew Prosecutor Lazare Matsocota, I came across him in Europe when he was studying law while I was doing a placement at the École Polytechnique de Vente in Paris. At that time Matsocota was president of the Association of Congolese Students in France, a brilliant man, he was so eloquent that sometimes when he spoke I would forget what I had to do that day, and just stay listening to him, like a pupil. They killed him, son! Like a rat! Like squashing a cockroach! Except that cockroaches are harmful, whereas I'd never seen so much humanity in one person as I did in Lazare Matsocota. The militia of Massamba-Débat's regime came to kidnap him at his home in Brazzaville and he wasn't the only one murdered on the night of the fourteenth of February, nineteen sixty-five: two more of our senior members of staff, former priest and director of the Congolese Information Agency, Anselme Massouémé, and first president of the Supreme Court in the Congo, Joseph Pouabou, were also executed, supposedly because they were plotting against the powers that be. Is that what you'd call politics, Jean-Pierre? No it is not!'

He looks really angry so the two other uncles pretend to be really angry too. I still don't get why he's talking to us about presidents from the past, instead of about Comrade President Marien Ngouabi. Uncle René could have been a magician, and I jump when he answers the question I asked in my head, even though no words actually came out of my mouth:

'So, Michel, this is where Comrade President Marien Ngouabi comes in … He's a northerner – young, lively, dynamic – fresh out of the Military Academy at Saint-Cyr, a member of the same political party as the southerner, Massamba-Débat, but he wants to shake up the way we do politics in this country. Ngouabi, who was a captain in the army at the time, disagrees with the policies of the Head of State, Massamba-Débat, who has him transferred to Pointe-Noire. But the captain refuses and is immediately put in prison and stripped of his rank. And so, just as the supporters of Patrice Lumumba in the Belgian Congo revolted when their leader was arrested, here the northerners and much of the military revolted to show that if Marien Ngouabi wasn't released, the country would be plunged into bloody havoc. President Massamba-Débat was forced to release Marien Ngouabi, and he was restored to the rank of captain. Now, when someone excites popular enthusiasm to that degree, people naturally think of him as heaven sent. And Marien Ngouabi was already set to take over running the country. So Massamba-Débat imprisoned him once again, because he talks too much, because he says what he thinks. This time he's rescued, along with other political prisoners, by para-commandos. Meanwhile, the president has to face the anger of the Lari, his own ethnic group, some of whom think Father Fulbert Youlou was better than him, and we're all set for another civil war …'

*

I'm half listening to him speaking, but half of me is also still wondering: Did he really come here with the two uncles I've never met just to tell me about stuff that happened before I was born and has nothing to do with the death of Marien Ngouabi?

Once again, as if by magic, Uncle René answers me:

'Michel. in a few minutes you'll see that everything I've told you up to now is directly linked to what is happening today ... So, President Massamba-Débat was in deep trouble with his ethnic group. He had also lost the confidence of the army; his commander of civil defence had even defected. Despite his attempts to save the situation, notably by forming a new government, Massamba-Débat was now no more than a rotting fruit at the mercy of the slightest wind. And that wind's name was Marien Ngouabi, who grew powerful at the heart of the National Movement for Revolution and the National Council for Revolution. The president had no choice but to resign, but young Ngouabi then recalled him to his duties by forming a new government, most of whose members were soldiers. Marien Ngouabi himself led the National Council for Revolution, his planned coup d'état took place peacefully: on the fourth of September nineteen sixty-eight, president Massamba-Débat is finally removed, the Prime Minister Alfred Raoul takes over the transition up to the first of January nineteen sixty-nine. No one is fooled; everyone knows that Marien Ngouabi's hour has come, and he will be our next president of the Republic. He will create the party I joined seven months ago, the Congolese Party of Labour. It was Marien Ngouabi who changed our national anthem, our flag, and who laid out the path of scientific socialism we follow today ...'

Maman Pauline reappears in the doorway with a plate

piled high with pieces of pineapple. She sets it down in the middle of the table.

'Still talking politics? I'm going back outside then ...'

Uncle René grabs her arm and holds her back.

'No, Pauline, you should sit down. I have some very bad news, very *very* bad news for all the family ...'

The list

Maman Pauline, Papa Roger and I are all really worried now. What does my uncle mean by 'very very bad news for all the family?'

My mother asks Uncle René:

'Have you got serious problems with the political crowd? I told you not to join the Party! You see what happens!'

'Pauline, we have some problems ...'

'What do you mean, "we"? Are we involved in their politics?'

'Pauline, listen to what Kinana and Moubéri have to say ...'

Uncle Moubéri begins:

'Well, sister, we had to run like rats when we heard the shots yesterday at fourteen thirty hours. I remember I was in my office preparing a report on the retirement of two white-collar workers when suddenly I heard, Ratatat! Ratatat! Ratatat! Ratatat! It was automatic-rifle fire coming from the direction of High Command, five hundred metres or so from our building, the National Social Savings Bank. Everyone knew the president had been living at High Command for the past eight years, so you can imagine the panic: pupils at the Patrice Lumumba High School close by running out of their class-rooms, taxis getting out of the area at breakneck speed, the shopkeepers all shutting up; basically the entire population was dashing that way and this, this way and that, but no one understood what had really happened. After nearly a quarter of an hour, which felt like an eternity, silence fell. Yes, Pauline, total silence! The radio had stopped transmitting, with no explanation – what could they tell us, when they themselves had received no orders? People had gathered on every floor of our building and were looking out of the windows over towards High Command. We heard rumours – some people said Zaire had just launched an attack against our army and we must prepare to counter-attack with arms that the government would supply. At that moment I went quickly back to my office to call brother Kinana at the Ministry for Rural Economy, to tell him something serious had happened and we needed to leave town as fast as possible …'

Uncle Kinana took up the story:

'In fact, sister Pauline, brother-in-law Roger, by the time Moubéri called me I already knew, because the Minister for Rural Economy had immediately quit the ministry, but instead of taking the official car he slipped past his drivers and bodyguards by dressing in ordinary clothes, with a straw hat as a disguise, then vanished into a bullet-proof car, which was waiting for him opposite the Ministry. He was in such a hurry that he left his briefcase behind in his office. He must have been very anxious; he didn't leave any precise instructions for us, his trusted advisors. My colleague, Prosper Okokima-Mokata, a northerner responsible for protocol, came bursting into my office and said – I quote verbatim: '"What the hell are you still doing here, Jean-Pierre? It's all over for Marien Ngouabi, he's had it! And it won't stop there; things are going to get worse from now on. You're a loyal man, I've always thought well of you, but if I was a loyal southerner like you I wouldn't hang around in Brazzaville a minute longer." I asked him what I should do, and just then I saw he was holding the briefcase the minister had left behind in his office. He opened it and said to me: "In here there are documents that lead me to think someone in your family is going to have problems, and wisdom teaches us that if you lose your ears it's time for your neck to start worrying!" There was a moment's silence, then he did me a favour for which I'll be grateful all my life. He said: "Go south, right now, Jean-Pierre. I can get you on a plane that leaves tomorrow for Pointe-Noire. After that it won't be possible; it will be the last one to take off from Brazzaville, the ceasefire will mean the total closure of all our borders and the imposition of a no-fly zone. I can give you the two tickets I was going to use for some trips I had coming up, and I guess that won't be a problem for you, since you're not married and don't have children ..." Just at that moment my phone rang: it was big brother Moubéri on the line ...'

Uncle Martin Moubéri took over next:

'So, after I'd made the call to little brother Jean-Pierre, I immediately called home to tell my wife and daughter to get out of the house, leave everything and go and hide out with the Singoumounas, a Lari family I've helped a lot by taking on the father and then the son at the National Social Savings Bank. From there this family put them in a truck that drove right across the Pool region and even as I speak they'll have reached our own region of Bouenza, where they will be safe with sister Dorothée Louhounou. After giving these instructions to my family I called brother René to let him know we'd be arriving the next day in Pointe-Noire, and he came to meet us at the airport ...'

Maman Pauline puts her elbows on the table and holds her head in her hands, as though she finds the whole story exhausting:

'René, what does all this have to do with us?'

Uncle René glances at the door and lowers his voice:

'Pauline, this assassination has created serious problems for our family. Today several soldiers and civilians from the south of the country have been arrested. They'll be brought before a court martial set up by the Military Committee of the Party, which is the new organ of the State. The ex-president of the Republic himself, Alphonse Massamba-Débat, is among those who will be judged by this court. They'll announce tomorrow who's on the Military Committee of the Party but the names of the eleven members are already doing the rounds in Brazzaville. So gradually they're setting up a military dictatorship, which will eliminate anyone who might talk because they know something about the assassination – though many people say you need look no further as the conspirators and assassins are among the eleven members of the Military Committee of the Party ...'

Maman Pauline, Papa Roger and I still don't see what my uncle's driving at. My mother doesn't work for the State, she's not a soldier. My father doesn't work for the State, he works for Madame Ginette, and Madame Ginette is a white who steers clear of problems, she's not involved in politics.

Uncle René continues:

'I have a photocopy of the document that was in the briefcase left behind by the Minister for Rural Economy when he fled. It says that the Military Committee of the Party "will faithfully continue the work of the Immortal Marien Ngouabi, leader of the Congolese Revolution, namely to build a socialist society in the Congo, according to the principles of Marxist-Leninism". Eye-wash! We all know how it will end: the members of the Military Committee of the Party will massacre each other, one lot will put the other lot in prison or

Uncle René nods at Uncle Martin Moubéri.

'Martin, get the document out of my briefcase ...'

Uncle Martin Moubéri presses a button on the briefcase and it opens with a click, which immediately gets our attention. He takes out several sheets of paper and selects one, which he unfolds before us. I can see some typewritten words, but I can't read them properly, everything's upside down. The only reason I recognise the name of ex-president Alphonse Massamba-Débat is because Uncle René's said it a lot this evening.

Uncle Moubéri hands the sheet of paper to Papa Roger, and he reads it in a low voice, as though he's praying at Saint-Jean-Bosco's. Uncle Moubéri didn't hand the sheet of paper to my mother first, because my mother can't read, though she's very good at speaking French, and at arithmetic, since she's a market trader.

Papa Roger suddenly places his finger on the sheet of paper, brings it up close to his nose and cries:

'NO! NO! NO! It's not true!'

Uncle René folds his arms and adopts an expression of sorrow.

'Yes, Roger, I'm afraid it is true.'

'But maybe this document—'

'This document is the real thing, Roger; it comes from a properly authorised source ...'

'But what do they have against the captain? What has he done to them?'

'He was up to his eyes in it.'

'Was?'

Uncle René doesn't reply. Uncle Kinana looks over at Uncle Martin Moubéri, then they both look at Uncle René, but all three of them avoid Maman Pauline and it's Uncle Martin who announces:

'Captain Luc Kimbouala-Nkaya was shot in cold blood yesterday at his home in the Plateau des Quinze-Ans neighbourhood of Brazzaville, by a group of militiamen, in the presence of his wife, his children and other members of the family—

Maman Pauline screams so loud my ears pop.

Papa Roger thumps the table with his fist and the grapefruit seeds rattle in my glass.

I thump the table too, and the wine glasses almost tip over and add more stains to our tired old tablecloth.

Out of all my uncles, Captain Luc Kimbouala-Nkaya was the one I knew best, apart from Uncle René and Uncle Mompéro, because Maman Pauline and I went to stay with him when Maman Pauline took me to visit Brazzaville for the first time. Oh, I was eight and a half years old and it was also the first time I'd travelled in the Micheline, the train that stops everywhere. We were lucky, there were no fatal derailments around the stations at Dolisie, Dechavanne, Mont Bélo, Hamon or Baratier; we arrived on time, that is to say a day and a half after we left. The station at Brazzaville was full of jostling people buying things that had been brought from Pointe-Noire. They didn't speak Munukutuba there, they spoke Lingala, and there weren't just Brazzavilians, there were people from Zaire as well, who'd crossed the river in canoes to get their hands on the produce. I saw trader women greet my mother respectfully. She responded by saying that she hadn't brought any bananas with her; she was taking me to spend my holidays with her brother Luc Kimbouala-Nkaya. As soon as they heard my uncle's name, they hunched themselves up small and were even more respectful to my mother. We took a green taxi, on to which had been loaded everything Maman

Pauline had brought to give Uncle Kimbouala-Nkaya: two white cockerels, two bunches of bananas, two large portions of peanut butter, ten maniocs she'd spent twenty-four hours in the kitchen preparing with her own hands, a little bag of cola nuts, two litres of corn liquor and two west-African tunics from the Grand Marché.

After a twenty-minute drive we arrived at the captain's home, which was guarded by two soldiers who treated us so respectfully, you'd have thought we were members of the Popular National Army. Uncle Kimbouala-Nkaya and his wife had killed a pig in our honour. That is the custom of the Babembe. We ate so well at my uncle's house that I told my mother I'd like to stay in Brazzaville for the rest of my life, in this fine, brick-built house, eating pigs when we had visitors. Also, because he was such a nice man, and didn't speak much, he let me try on his beret in front of the mirror in the living room, where I would take up a military stance and shout: 'Atten-shun!' He was kind, but you had to be careful not to overstep the mark. His children and I knew we weren't allowed to touch the gun hidden in a locked case. My uncle kept the key in his pocket, or my cousins would start World War Three, some of them hiding behind the house, others in the neighbours' yards.

I first watched television at Uncle Kimbouala-Nkaya's, and I'll never forget it, because the whole household stayed up till dawn to watch the fight beamed in from Zaire. We saw Muhammad Ali fight George Foreman at the 20th of May Stadium, and each time Ali hit Foreman in the face we cheered and chanted, 'Kill him, Ali! Ali, *boma ye*! Ali, *boma ye*!'

Uncle Kimbouala-Nkaya's house was very fine. Even though it wasn't finished, it wasn't like the 'houses in waiting', because the captain kept on with the building work – he had enough money to finish everything sooner or later. Everyone in the Plateau des Quinze-Ans neighbourhood envied this house. Before you arrived in the inner courtyard, you had to walk down a long corridor, and along this corridor there were rooms which any member of the family could stay in when they passed through Brazzaville. I remember there were three rooms on one side and three on the other. At the end of the corridor into the little circular inner courtyard was a wonderful light, as if God Himself had lit the house. All around this inner courtyard, Uncle Kimbouala-Nkaya had built four apartments, and the one he lived in with his wife was the one facing you as you came in, the biggest and lightest of all. In this room there was a shower, like in the Victory Palace Hotel, and toilets, again like in the Victory Palace Hotel, so you had to take care because as soon as you'd finished what you had to do in there you had to pull on a chain to flush away whatever had come out of your belly, which I won't describe here, or people will say oh Michel always exaggerates and that sometimes he says rude things without meaning to …

'What really happened, René?' my father asked. Uncle René empties his glass.

'Like I told you, Roger, it's a witch-hunt against the southerners in the National Popular Army. And it's not just the military: Cardinal Biayenda, a Lari, has already been arrested, and he's a man of God. They'll do the same to him as they did to the captain, and it'll be the same for ex-president Alphonse Massamba-Débat. All the names on the list I showed you will go the same way, and their families …'

When Maman Pauline hears these words she quickly wipes her tears with the edge of her wrap.

'So you're telling me these wicked soldiers from Brazzaville are going to come to my house and murder me right in front of Michel, like they murdered my brother in front of his wife and children?'

Uncle René shakes his head – for yes or for no? I can't tell.

'Pauline, it depends ... How will people know we are related to the Kimbouala-Nikayas, since we don't have the same family name?'

Maman Pauline is almost yelling at my uncles Kinana and Moubéri:

'Why couldn't my brother come with you yesterday in your plane? Why did they kill our brother? Tell, me – why?'

After a pause, Uncle René answers:

'Pauline, I always had the feeling that Captain Kimbouala-Nkaya was aware of the terrible fate awaiting him, but even though he knew, he wasn't someone to draw back from death. His whole life was like that, courageously lived, and we have just lost one of the greatest Babembe soldiers ever to serve this country ...'

Uncle René tells us that the captain went to the Military School at Saint-Cyr with Louis Sylvain-Goma, who is now a member of the Military Committee of the Party. He says this school in Saint-Cyr is really famous, all soldiers dream of being trained over there in France. The captain had met other Congolese during his training, in particular Comrade President Marien Ngouabi and Joachim Yhombi-Opango, who had also joined the Military Committee of the Party.

When Uncle René explains all this, we begin to realise how small the world is, and that Uncle Kimbouala-Nkaya knew most of the people on the Military Committee of the Party, or maybe it was them that knew him and had reason to fear him. We all thought we knew the captain, but we knew nothing about him. Maman Pauline never told me the whole story about him. And besides, since she didn't go to school how could she understand that the school at Saint-Cyr isn't like the Three-Glorious-Days or the Karl Marx Lycée? That's why I listen with all ears when Uncle René tells us that after his training at Saint-Cyr the captain came back to this country and was given the job of training future soldiers to safeguard our Congolese Socialist Revolution. He did such a good job that he was transferred here to Pointe-Noire and put in charge of the soldiers. But I wasn't born then, and Maman Pauline was living in Mouyondzi, in the Bouenza region. Uncle René, back from his training in France, and Uncle Albert, who had been taken on by the National Electricity Board, were the only ones who used to go and see the captain in Military Zone 2, where he was in charge. Uncle Kimbouala-Nkaya was such a good worker that he ended up as Chief of Staff. But when the regime of President Alphonse Massamba-Débat fell, they sacked Uncle Kimbouala-Nkaya from his post and replaced him with Louis Sylvain-Goma, the one who'd been a comrade of his at Saint-Cyr, the one who's now on the Military Committee of the Party.

Again I think about how all these people knew each other. Especially when Uncle René reveals that even after Uncle Kimbouala-Nkaya had been sacked, he was called back to create the National Council of the Revolution, along with other soldiers including Marien Ngouabi, who wasn't yet our president, and Denis Sassou-Nguesso and Louis Sylvain-Goma, who are both now members of the Military Committee of the Party. Uncle Kimbouala-Nkaya also went on to help create our Congolese Party of Labour, which is like the baby of the National Council of the Revolution. The captain was starting to work his way back up through the ranks when comrade Marien Ngouabi became president of the Republic: by this time he was deputy political commissioner of the Army, alongside

Ange Diawara, former Commander of Civil Defence, and ex-president Alphonse Massamba-Débat. My uncle and Ange Diawara were great friends. They got on really well; they both wanted our country to work. That's why they were outspoken in criticising the tribalism that appeared to surround Comrade President Marien Ngouabi. Because he said too much, criticised too much, the captain was sacked by Comrade President Marien Ngouabi. On 22 February 1972, Uncle René says, the captain's close friend Ange Diawara launched a coup d'état against Comrade President Marien Ngouabi but it failed. Our uncle was in immediate danger, being too close to Diawara. He was put in prison, condemned to death with other politicians thought to be part of the plot.

Uncle René is sweating, he's talked too much. He takes out a white tissue and wipes his brow.

'Captain Kimbouala-Nkaya and the other so-called accomplices in the coup d'état were not killed, they were pardoned by Comrade President Marien Ngouabi … Five years later – that is yesterday, 18 March 1977 – only a few hours after the assassination of Comrade President Marien Ngouabi, a group of military men went to our brother's house to arrest him, on the pretext that he was either intimately or loosely involved with the plotters. And during the course of his arrest, he was killed in cold blood …'

Uncle René's stopped talking. He looks at each of us in turn, as though trying to assess how sad, but most of all, how angry we are.

Maman Pauline asks again:

'Does this mean that the military from Brazzaville are going to come and handcuff us and take us to the Côte Sauvage to be killed at five in the morning?'

'Pauline, I've already told you, we don't have the same name.

You're Kengué; I'm Mabahou; Mompéro's Mvoundou! Who's going to know we are all children of Grégoire Massengo?'

'But practically speaking, René, what should we do?' asks Papa Roger as everyone starts to get up from the table, and my uncle turns back his jacket collar.

Uncle René addresses my mother:

'I have to ask for your total discretion; you never know. That's why Moubéri and Kinana have left Brazzaville, where they were too exposed. I'm going to keep them at my house for the time being ... For now, Pauline, there must be no trading, and no trips to the bush. If you need money I'll give you some from time to time, but I want you to stop travelling, the trains are full of soldiers, and they check everything ...'

Hearing all this, Maman Pauline sobs even louder. She goes off into her bedroom and I know she's gone to weep real tears now, a flood of hot tears, because this business has touched the thing she loves most: her trade in bananas. And when I think of the flood of hot tears coursing down her cheeks I want to go into my room too, I can feel myself beginning to cry. I'll weep like Maman Pauline weeps, not just because my mother's business has been ruined by Comrade President Marien Ngouabi's death, not just because Uncle Kimbouala-Nkaya has been assassinated in front of his wife and children, but also, and no one here knows this, because I still can't understand why my dog hasn't come back home when there's a curfew on, and he may be in danger somewhere out in this sad city, that lies so silent this Saturday night, 19 March 1977, when each of us stands alone, quite alone.

A car engine starts up outside. Uncle René's left, taking my two uncles with him ...

Sand in my eyes

I can hear my parents' voices. Normally at this hour, if we hadn't had a bucket-load of bad news, they'd already be snoring away. But they're arguing about something that bothers me: Maman Pauline is telling Papa Roger that she's going to shave her head, so she'll have a total skinhead like women do when a member of their family's just died. They keep their head shaved for one month, minimum. As soon as it grows just a few millimetres they shave it again, and when you stroke their heads it's like cement, all smooth and clean. Every day these women mark a cross on the wall, and once they get to thirty crosses, they know it's been a month already and soon they'll stop shaving because the mourning is over and no one will mind now if they're beautiful, they don't have to stay ugly till the corpse of their loved one's rotted away. While they're in mourning they're not allowed to dance, wear lipstick, nail polish or make-up. It's only after a month they can do that, a little bit at a time, because if they make themselves exciting and delicious all of a sudden the dead person will be cross and refuse to rot away in the ground. If they don't rot it's dangerous for everyone: he'll come back and complain every night in the dreams of the people in the family, and he'll be seen weeping with his back pressed up against a tree that's lost most of its leaves and has stopped giving fruit.

That's why Papa Roger doesn't want my mother to shave her head:

'Pauline if you shave your head people will think there's been a death in the family and—'

'So?'

'Well, then people round here are going to ask where the corpse is, so they can chip in and support you! Is that what you want?'

'Roger, I am going to shave my head!'

'No, you must stay natural, discreet, as though nothing had happened!'

'What do you mean, as though nothing had happened? My brother's been murdered by the northerners!'

'Listen to me, Pauline. I feel your pain, but we need to be careful.'

'So I'm not meant to weep for my brother, is that it? I'll never see his body?'

'That's not what I'm saying, but I'd be surprised if they allow anyone to organise a funeral in Brazzaville for someone they were so keen to get rid of ...'

'All right then, I'll make the northerners I know pay for what they did to my brother!'

'Pauline ...'

'I'll make them pay, I swear it! Just who do they think they are?'

'I see. So you're going to get a gun and go and mow down the members of the Military Committee of the Party, one after the other. Be realistic!'

'On Monday I'll go to the market and if the stall holder who's owed me money for months now doesn't pay back the whole lot, I'll teach her not to mess with Pauline Kengué, daughter of Grégoire Massengo and Henriette Nsoko!

Then she really will see I'm the younger sister of Captain Kimbouala-Nkaya!'

'That's not a good idea. The northerner you're talking about isn't just anyone, you know she's not, she's a member of the Revolutionary Union of Congolese Women—'

'What? So when those people in Brazzaville decided to kill my brother, that was a good idea, was it? Because my brother *was* just anyone, is that what you're saying?'

'You mustn't go to see that woman, Pauline, especially not alone and—'

'I'll go with Michel then! In any case, you'll be sleeping at your other wife, Martine's house, that's all you think of at the moment; I don't even know what you're doing here right now!'

'Now you're just bringing up things that have nothing to do with what we're talking about, Pauline …'

'Are you trying to make me believe you're not happy you're going back to see Martine? You're not happy to be seeing your real children? Why don't you just go now, are you afraid of the curfew too?'

She's crying; my father comforts her, begs her not to cut her hair, not to go to the market to pick a fight with the northern stall holder who isn't just anyone. I think to myself that my mother's not just anyone either. She is the daughter of Grégoire Massengo, who was head of the village of Louboulou.

Maman Pauline's sobs gradually subside and no one's speaking in my parents' bedroom now. I feel like there's sand in my eyes that I can't get rid of. I keep rubbing at them. I yawn, and feel really weak, I can't move my hands or my feet, as though I've been tied to the bed. The house starts spinning, spinning on its own axis, slowly at first, then really fast, just at the moment my eyes close …

Sunday 20 March 1977

The Voice of the Congolese Revolution

Papa Roger doesn't want to listen to the Voice of the Congolese Revolution this morning, he's tuned into Voice of America. He thinks the Americans are the only people who know what's happening in the world. When you think you know about the news before they do they burst out laughing, because they have tiny tape recorders, the size of a grain of corn, which they hide in the houses of the presidents of Africa who are going to get assassinated. So today I'm not surprised when they give out loads of details that our Congolese journalists can't know because they don't have hidden tape recorders the size of a grain of corn. The Voice of the Congolese Revolution is still waiting for the Military Committee of the Party to let them know what they're meant to report about the fact that our Comrade President Marien Ngouabi was bumped off on 18 March at 14.30, a time when normally people are having their siesta because it's so hot everywhere. If the Military Committee of the Party began saying that Comrade President Marien Ngouabi had done a Jesus and resurrected, as if death was just like a mini siesta, the Congolese journalists would repeat it without checking. But as the Military Committee of the Party still haven't said anything, the Voice of the Congolese Revolution just carry on broadcasting Soviet military songs that make me dream of snow and Soviet soldiers marching on snow but not getting cold feet because they have special boots, which our soldiers will never have because we don't have snow over here.

Every now and then they played old speeches by the deceased leader of the Revolution, and Papa Roger got fed up and switched over to listen to American radio where the journalists speak in French especially for us Africans.

Another thing that irritated Papa Roger on our national radio was a journalist with a voice like an alcoholic telling all these stories about Marien Ngouabi's life as though he had lived with him or had actually been there on the day our leader of the Revolution was born. He wept as he told us that our leader of the Revolution wasn't the son of rich folk, that he was poor, like most Congolese, and born in a little village, called Ombellé way up in the north. It was a real bush village, the kind you only ever find in books by white people talking about blacks, with a few huts and where everyone knows everyone else because they're all related and they all have children with each other without worrying about having babies with deformities like a boar's mouth or pig's feet. Also, in this village called Ombellé there actually are pigs that just hang around all day because they've got nothing to do but eat poop and wait for the day when they'll be eaten or sold. In this village, Ombellé, there are also cockerels who always get the time wrong, and go cock-a-doodle-doo at midday, thinking that will make night-time come, when they should be going cock-a-doodle-doo at dawn, so the peasants won't be late to go and weed the fields and plant sweet potatoes and taros and yams. No one can ask God to be born in Ombellé, but this journalist with a voice like an alcoholic said that it was the most beautiful village in the world and that on 31 December 1938, the baby they called Marien Ngouabi, only son of

Maman Mboualé Abemba and Dominique Osséré m'Opoma could not have been born in any other place, or he'd never have become our comrade president of the Republic! The ancestors had decreed it, they were present at the birth, and really excited, blessing the baby, telling him to tread carefully in life because nothing's a straight line, to be truly good and just till the day he died. Apparently the angels were zipping up and down between up there and down here, to check that they hadn't given the wrong baby this mega important mission.

In this village, the journalist with the voice of an alcoholic continued, the children can go fishing and hunting once they turn seven, as if they were adults. They know how to make traps to catch birds and mice and our comrade president was already really smart at all that, he wasn't afraid of the dark, had no fear of devils, ghosts, snake or other beasts that usually scare children of his age. He spent his childhood in this remote spot, then went to primary school a few kilometres away, in a town called Owando – if a tiny village like Ombellé had a school there would only be two or three people in the class because up there all you find is a few old people with white beards sweeping their floors and old people don't go to school. The journalist with the voice of an alcoholic even swore by Almighty God that when he crossed the River Koyo to go to school little Marien Ngouabi refused the help of the boatmen, and chose to swim across himself. At this point I wondered why he didn't explain how Marien Ngouabi managed not to get his school books wet while swimming, or how come he never got eaten up mid-stream by dangerous crocodiles. Perhaps the ancestors protected him and the crocodiles became all nice and friendly and helped him to get to the other side of the river before the boatmen, and the crocodiles actually waited for him there to bring him back to the other side after school.

The journalist with the voice of an alcoholic had told us that it was clear that young Marien Ngouabi was going to become an important man, because he'd been class leader and captain of the football team in his primary school. And at this point our journalist friend told us a secret about the youth of the defunct comrade president, to prove to the doubters that he was brave even as a boy, and that death did not frighten him. He told the tale in some detail:

The president was in middle school, just turned fourteen. One day the pupils were bathing in the River Koyo, where the waters were high, when suddenly there was uproar right across the river. 'A child is drowning! A child is drowning! In the beginners' class!' As the bathers scrambled hastily from the water, updates on the situation came thick and fast: 'A crocodile's snatched the child!' Who will risk their life to save the child as he struggles weakly, caught in the dark currents of the powerful River Koyo? Before a terrified crowd, scorning wind and weather, young Marien Ngouabi flings himself into the water, swims quickly over to the child, who actually is drowning, grabs hold of him and returns victorious with him to the riverbank, to the great satisfaction of all concerned. In fact, the child pulled from the water was not from the same village as young Ngouabi. He was a pupil at the school in Elinginawe, the next village on from Owando, son of Olouengué, a little boy named Olouengué François. In 1976 President Marien Ngouabi granted an audience to this 'Moses', now a full-grown man and a history teacher at one of our country's lycées. And this meeting took place in the presence of our current Minister for Foreign Affairs, Théophile Obenga, whose poignant account I read word for word, and which is indelibly printed in the memory of the Congolese people, because it's part of our history too ...

Then the journalist said something about little Marien

Ngouabi's studies at the Military Preparatory school Général-Leclerc in Brazzaville, after his Certificate of Primary and Elementary Studies. I myself was able to go to the Three-Glorious-Days because I got this qualification, and I'm going to try really hard for the Karl Marx Lycée, which is close to the sea, and where I'll be able to watch the white cranes 'fly above us, moaning as they go'. Little Marien Ngouabi, on the other hand, did not go to the Three-Glorious-Days, but to Général-Leclerc, which, according to the journalist, has become the school for Young Revolutionaries, and they are the ones who'll go on to be leaders of the country, because they're already learning to be soldiers. From here he went to Oubangi-Chari, where he became a sergeant. Next he went off to Cameroon with the French Army. Papa Roger whispered something to me that the journalist hadn't said, but was very important: the French army was massacring the poor Cameroonians, who were demanding independence, and during these massacres, aided by the Cameroonian army, a man had been killed who was as important as Patrice Lumumba, whose name was Ruben Um Nyobè. This great man opposed colonisation; he wanted independence for his country. He was caught because the Africans actually told the whites where he was hiding in the scrubland, and the militiamen first shot him down then dishonoured his body, dragging it about, so it scraped on the ground, and getting him so covered in mud you couldn't even recognise him as Ruben Um Nyobè.

The journalist then explained that the situation was such that young Marien Ngouabi wanted to resign from being a soldier but he couldn't because first he had to pay back to the French army the money he'd been lent for his studies, and like most students his pockets, even though they were deep army-issue pockets, were empty. So he stayed in the French army, who put him in with the Cameroonians of the Bamiléké group. These Cameroonians are the most stubborn fighters, you don't mess with them, they don't care if their enemies are white or black, they defend their territory and the people of their ethnic group to the death, even with spoons, forks and water laced with chilli pepper. After his time with the Bamilékés, he was sent to Douala, then finally left Cameroon to come back here, to Owando, which is near his home village of Ombellé. Just after our independence, on 15 August 1969, the young soldier was sent to the military training school in Strasbourg. So he went to France, and was accepted at the Military Academy of Saint-Cyr, for officer training. It was at Saint-Cyr that he met my Uncle Kimbouala-Nkaya and other members of the current Military Committee of the Party and while he was there he fell in love with a French woman, Clotilde Martin, a waitress in a tea shop, with whom he had two children, Roland Ngouabi and Marien Ngouabi Junior (which didn't mean the comrade president loved him more than Roland, just so as not to get him mixed up with the leader of the Congolese Revolution because there's only one Marien Ngouabi in this world).

The idea was that Clotilde Martin would become his wife, but she got very annoyed and decided to go back and live in her own country because Comrade President Ngouabi had taken a second wife called Céline Mvouka, who we called Maman Céline Ngouabi. The journalist with the voice of an alcoholic explained that his marriage to Clotilde Martin didn't bother the Congolese because it was good to show that we weren't racist, that we can marry white women of all different kinds and even embrace them as our national *maman*, whereas Uncle Pompidou was unlikely to leave his white wife, today or tomorrow, for a nice big black woman from our country, or even keep his white wife and add in another one, black as the day she was born, and make all the French exclaim: 'What's going on?' The journalist was quick to point out that back in 1962, when the young Marien Ngouabi married Clotilde Martin, the poor waitress didn't realise she'd married a man who would later become comrade president of the Republic, and that she'd become our national white *maman*. So people who went round spreading stories, such as that the white woman had taken advantage of the situation, were idiots who didn't understand that it's not written on a baby's brow that they're going to be president, that would just create all sorts of problems for the baby and they'd spend their childhood dealing with jealous people and people trying to make money by saying they were related and stuff like that. The journalist also said that when he got back here after independence in 1963, young Lieutenant Marien Ngouabi was living in Pointe-Noire, as a military commander, just like my Uncle Kimbouala-Nkaya. Five years later, because of all the troubles in our country, Lieutenant Marien Ngouabi became too famous, he made the president, Alphonse Massamba-Débat, step down and became comrade president of the Republic himself …

The journalist from the Voice of the Congolese Revolution didn't explain it all as well as my Uncle René did. He missed out dates and names because he knew the Military Committee of the Party always listens to the radio and can ask for everything to be cut and the whole story to be retold the way it wants it. Also, while he was telling us all this, his story was constantly being interrupted by reports from the spokesman for the Military Committee of the Party, a man called Florent Ntsiba, who is from an ethnic group in the interior of our country. I recognised his voice because it was the same one that had announced the day before yesterday:

Now, with its back to the wall and in its death throes, imperialism has used a suicide unit to launch a cowardly attack on the life of our dynamic leader of the Congolese Revolution, Comrade Marien Ngouabi, who died in combat with his weapon in his hand, this Friday, 18 March 1977, at 14:30 hours.

The last report we heard before we finally switched stations was when the spokesman, Florent Ntsiba, announced what the Military Committee of the Party had said to the foreign ambassadors who were also trying to figure out how Comrade President Marien Ngouabi came to die. He read without drawing breath, as if war had come within an arm's length of the River Congo and we needed to prepare to take up arms:

Gentlemen Ambassadors and Heads of Diplomatic Service,

In the name of the Military Committee of the Party set up last night by the Central Committee of the Congolese Party of Labour, invested with all necessary powers and on behalf of the government, it is our sad duty to announce to you the brutal death of Comrade Marien Ngouabi, President of the Republic, President of the Central Committee of the Congolese Party of Labour and Head of State. The killing of the leader of the Congolese Revolution, perpetrated by imperialism and its lackeys, occurred on Friday 18 March 1977 at 14:30 hours, at the official residence of the General Staff. This heinous crime was committed by ex-captain Barthélemy Kikadidi. Two members of the commando unit were killed and two others, including ex-captain Barthélemy Kikadidi are on the run—

At this point Papa Roger switched off the radio, even before we'd finished listening to the report, and told me he was only listening to the Voice of the Congolese Revolution because he needed to know what the instructions were for the period of national mourning, not to listen to explanations that no one was going to take seriously, because there was no proof and had been no investigation, and already they were giving out the names of people they were trying to catch even before they secretly crossed the borders into countries like Zaire, Gabon or Cameroon.

On the Voice of the Congolese Revolution we didn't learn anything about the period of national mourning, but I wouldn't expect it to be a normal kind of mourning, where the women totally shave their heads, and people go and drink coffee, meet up with girls, and take their mats outside to sleep beside the corpse, which is kept in a palm leaf store. We can't expect that, because we don't have the body with us, we can't sleep beside it till the day of the burial. The body is somewhere back in Brazzaville. Why would you mourn someone when you haven't actually got the dead person in front of you?

Since we had no instructions, people just said what they felt like saying. Everyone wants a proper mourning period, and some people are saying we should wear a piece of black material on our right arm, even so, so people out in the street can see we're sad. Other people say that anyone seen crying a lot will be in favour with the Military Committee of the Party, while people who don't cry at all will have big problems. They also say that music in the bars shouldn't be played too loud; it should be mostly traditional songs from the different ethnic groups, not rumbas by Franco or Tabu Ley or hits from Papa Wemba or Zaiko Langa Langa, because their rhythms are too upbeat when people are in mourning. Flags mustn't be raised to the top of the mast and they mustn't fly just any old how, even if there's a wind. Friday 19 March, they announced on the radio, was a paid holiday. That means people are paid even if they don't go to work. We also heard that people who worked in State offices were returning to work on Monday and apparently they are required to wear a black cloth round their right arm in the office. The borders with the countries that surround us are now closed. This also means that no one can come into the country, and no one can leave it, except for the members of the Congolese Party of Labour, who have to show their round red badges that make me think of Father Weyler's wafers at Saint-Jean-Bosco's during catechism.

School is closed till Tuesday; there are no classes till Wednesday. We can go out during the day but we have to be home by seven o'clock and stay there till seven in the morning or get whipped by the police with a Motobécane AV42 drive chain …

Voice of America

So now Papa Roger and I are listening to Voice of America, and it's all quite different. There are two journalists commenting on the bad news of two days ago, a woman and a man, but it's the woman who's in charge, because she always asks the difficult questions and the man answers like a pupil who's learned his times tables, or maybe he knows everything about our country because he's lived in Brazzaville and works for this woman, who I imagine being very tall, very beautiful, with high heels like the ones Maman Pauline wears when she goes into town and drops in to say hello to Papa Roger at the Victory Palace Hotel, so my father can see she's an elegant woman with her wrap knotted tightly about her and gold-plated earrings, which do look like gold from a distance.

The journalist asks the man who knows everything about our country:

So, Christopher Smith, you've been watching the political situation in Africa at first hand, what's your analysis of the present situation in Brazzaville?

Christopher is only too happy to be asked this question and to have it pointed out that he's often in Africa and has worked there for years. It is also pointed out that he has been in several places where there were civil wars on this continent, and that he's written a big book with lots of evidence inside, evidence that explains how the people who colonised us are often hiding behind us, selling us arms and getting us to fight each other.

Instead of talking directly about our problems, which right now are extremely serious, Christopher Smith goes round in circles like a truck warming up its engine before setting off:

Well, Sophie, as discussed in detail in my book Night Falls over Africa, *political assassinations on the dark continent have become a sinister tradition in the years since the first steps towards independence in the early sixties, from the start, in fact, of the movements to liberate Africa from the yoke of the western colonisers …*

And he throws in names, dates, explanations, which our journalists could never provide. But maybe all that is already in his book, whose title he mentions rather a lot. I'm very surprised to hear how well he pronounces the name of our prophet André Grenard Matsoua, and I'm also proud that he calls him a 'politician'. He says Matsoua was a stubborn man who faced up to the colonisers. He'd attended the seminary, the school of the whites, and worked for the customs office in Brazzaville and joined the French army to fight in Morocco against a dreadful resistance fighter called Abd el-Krim, who the colonisers lost sleep over because he was winning battles against the Spanish, the French and the British! And it's thanks to men like André Grenard Matsoua that these countries were able to save a bit of face, because they fought for them!

Christopher Smith carries on:

Sophie, no one denies that Matsoua added his own stone to the edifice of the French empire. He was captain of the one of the black regiments in the colonial army, the 22nd, known as the Senegalese Tirailleurs, though not only Senegalese served in it, but Congolese too, like Matsou! Sadly he died in prison, where he had been sent to do forced labour by the same colonial administration under which he'd served, he was becoming a significant voice, representing hope – and danger. The obscure circumstances of his death added to his growing reputation as a prophet and influenced the people of Pool, the Lari region he originally came from, to the point where, even today, thirty-five years after his death and seven years after the death of General de Gaulle, who was president in his day and much loved by the Lari, there are still people originating from Pool who go and wait at Brazzaville airport for these two people to return. The Lari are convinced that the prophet Matsoua and General de Gaulle aren't dead, that's just a lie put about by the French, and that these two men, who were not ordinary mortals like us, will return, sooner or later, that they'll be seen stepping off the plane, will wave to the crowd who've come to welcome them, and the General will go back to govern France and the prophet Matsoua will do miracles and heal the lame, the blind and infertile women. General de Gaulle is so much in the minds of the Lari that they have a cult of Ngoul, a fetish they worship and who represents the General, with a long nose and a cap with stars on ...

Next the American journalist comes out with the name of the Cameroonian Ruben Um Nyobè, who Papa Roger talked to me about when we still used to listen to the Voice of the Congolese Revolution, which hadn't mentioned this bit even though this man was as important as Patrice Lumumba. Christopher Smith has lots of details: Ruben Um Nyobè was assassinated on 13 September 1958 by a black soldier, Paul Abdoulaye, originally from Chad, who was even decorated by the French.

He talks about another Cameroonian called Félix Moumié, who was poisoned by the French secret services in a Swiss restaurant and died three days later on 3 November 1960. This was another man who wanted independence for his country.

At this point I start to think that it's really not OK to kill people in Swiss restaurants, because Papa Roger used to support the Swiss football team and wanted the English to be thrashed in the semi-final of the World Cup by the Swiss, who can buy off the referees because it has banks with masses of huge banknotes that have been really well laundered and ironed with a clothes iron so they stay nice and clean and flat.

There are too many dates coming up now; Christopher Smith's getting in a muddle himself, and each time he contradicts what he's just said. First he says Patrice Lumumba was assassinated on 7 January 1961, then he corrects it to 17 January 1961. On 13 January 1963 it was Sylvanus Olympio's turn to be assassinated; he was the first president the Togolese had chosen themselves, like people choose in developed countries. And it was the first time, Christopher Smith tells us, that an African president had been murdered after independence. Sylvanus Olympio was replaced by the former prime minister, Nicolas Grunitzky, but there's someone impatient lining up to launch another coup d'état: his name is Etienne Eyadéma, he was one of the militiamen who went to look for Sylvanus Olympio in the American embassy, where he had gone into hiding because even presidents are afraid of dying. Eyadéma has now been in power for over ten years ...

And there's more: on 29 October 1965, Mehdi Ben Barka was condemned to death in his own country, Morocco. He was kidnapped outside a restaurant in France, a bit like the Cameroonian Félix Moumié in Switzerland. Apparently the body of Mehdi Ben Barka has never been found and it's pretty sure the secret services of France and Morocco conspired to assassinate him.

Only four years ago, on 20 January 1973, Christopher Smith continues, it was the turn of the father of independence in Guinea Bissau and Cap Vert, Amilcar Cabral, to be killed , this time far away in Guinea Conakry, at the hand of his own party, who had plotted with their colonisers, the Portuguese. According to the man who knows everything, Guinea Conakry were also involved, because the president of that country, Ahmed Sékou Touré, had covered over the traces so no one would know how the assassination had been done. Amilcar Cabral sadly never saw Guinea Bissau and Cap Vert, which he loved with all his heart, gain independence: he died six months before it happened ...

And lastly, dear Sophie, as we recall these macabre episodes, let us not forget that on 26 August 1973, Outel Bono of Chad, who opposed the regime of François Tombalbaye, was killed in central Paris, with two shots from a revolver ...

Christopher Smith now returns to the subject of the death of Comrade President Marien Ngouabi. According to him there are two possible explanations; one is the one that the Military Committee of the Party gave; the other is the one given by Marien Ngouabi Junior, one of the two mixed-race sons Comrade President Marien Ngouabi had with Clotilde Martin ...

But before I put forward these two versions, dear Sophie, allow me to put things in context ...

And off he goes again with his muddled-up dates. He says that on 22 February 1972, so five years ago, there had been a previous attempt on Comrade President Marien Ngouabi's life by the soldier Ange Diawara, who was a close colleague of my Uncle Kimbouala-Nkaya. Ange Diawara had conspired with some members of the Congolese Party of Labour who were unhappy about the policies of our Revolutionary leader. Up until then Ange Diawara had been a normal man, studying economics like Uncle Kinana at the Lumumba University in the USSR. With the sudden arrival in our country of the Socialist Revolution, Ange Diawara became an important figure in the presidential guard of our former president Massamba-Débat, the one who is currently on the list of the people the Military Committee of the Party doesn't like and who are definitely heading for execution, like Uncle Kimbouala-Nkaya.

So, when Comrade President Marien Ngouabi, who in 1964 was not yet president, fell out with President Massamba-Débat, Ange Diawara took Captain Marien Ngouabi's side, and betrayed his own leader, President Massamba-Débat. He became a very high-up person in the military once Captain Marien Ngouabi came to power. People were afraid of Ange Diawara, not just because he was a soldier, but also because he was unbeatable at karate. Ange Diawara was present when Comrade President Marien Ngouabi founded the Congolese Party of Labour and had also taken up a post as Minister for Water and Forestry in the government of Comrade President Marien Ngouabi. But the problem with him was he kept criticising the Revolutionary leader because in his view things weren't going the way the people wanted, and everything was still expensive, like under the European capitalists: manioc, potatoes, sugar, palm and ground nut oil, oil – even though we have oodles of it – none of it was any cheaper for people to buy. Now it wasn't Comrade President Marien Ngouabi's fault that oil was so expensive, it was because the Arab countries, who also have oodles of oil, keep changing the prices to upset Europe, and we are unfortunately obliged to raise our prices, forgetting that that also makes problems for our own people, who have to put out their storm lanterns before they go to sleep, to save oil. And another thing, even after the Socialist

Revolution and communism, there was still too much tribalism, while the bellies of the ministers got bigger and bigger from eating up all the State's money and not giving any to ordinary folk. Because Ange Diawara said things without fear of the president, school pupils and students backed him, and said he was the real revolutionary, not Comrade President Marien Ngouabi. Ange Diawara encouraged school pupils and students everywhere to go on strike against the government. Would Comrade President Marien Ngouabi really keep on a Minister for Water and Forestry under such conditions? No! He sacked him, like a worker who keeps turning up late to the office or on site, and Diawara said: 'I don't care about being sacked; I'm going to hold a coup d'état.' And that's what he began to cook up.

Comrade President Marien Ngouabi was in Pointe-Noire on an official visit when Ange Diawara launched his coup d'état in Brazzaville. Our Revolutionary leader was as smart as a kingfisher: he immediately cancelled his official visit and took a plane to go and call time on this mayhem. As a result, our president, who was meant to be assassinated on 22 February 1972, escaped death by the skin of his teeth. The army captured and killed lots of Diawara's friends, people he was in the resistance with in the Pool region. During this period the finest musician in our country, Franklin Boukaka, was also caught and liquidated. He was a kind man and didn't sing to get people to dance and get all sweaty in bars, he sang about good things like peace between north and south, between Laris and Tékés, Bembés and Mbochis, and all the ethnic groups we have in our country which have nothing better to do than squabble among themselves as if there wasn't work to be getting on with in our towns and in our fields. Meanwhile they had killed the nice musician, Franklin Boukaka, so now

Ange Diawara was fleeing to Zaire where he'd found this place to hide. He could even have stayed there, become a Zairian among Zairians and have a Zairian wife and children, etc., but they trapped him like a child lured in by iced sweets like the ones Ma Moubobi sells; they promised to have talks with him, said he could come back to talk things over, and he fell for their lies. They arrested him as soon as he got back to Brazzaville, with his beard, which had grown incredibly long, as if the spirits of our ancestors had been watering it with invisible hands. He was whizzed over to headquarters, and there – Bam! Bam! Bam! Bam! – he and some of his friends were all shot. But as people didn't believe they could kill a powerful, mystical and invincible guy like Ange Diawara, who was a karate expert, they had to give proof. Which is why the government displayed their bodies at the Revolutionary Stadium, and no one was in any doubt, because everyone could see now that there was no magic, it really was the corpses of Ange Diawara and his friends laid out there like salt cod for sale at Ma Moubobi's, except they hadn't put salt on their bodies. So that was the end of poor Ange Diawara ...

I like all the details Christopher gives when he tells us about what Comrade President Marien Ngouabi did that day, when the Voice of the Congolese Revolution doesn't know about it yet. First of all, in the morning, our Revolutionary leader went to the university to give a lesson in physics and chemistry because he liked passing on his learning for free to young people. In the afternoon he went back to his presidential office to welcome some very important people, including Cardinal Emile Biayenda, who, like ex-president Massamba-Débat, is on the list of people the new leaders plan to liquidate. Cardinal Emile Biayenda is the archbishop of Brazzaville. He's only fifty years old, so compared to the other cardinals he's still young. On the radio they say Pope Paul VI chose him as a cardinal, and it's the first time we've had a cardinal in our country. He'd gone to the headquarters to meet Comrade President Marien Ngouabi because he had a favour to ask him: for a while now he'd been worried that the Patrice Lumumba Lycée was getting bigger and bigger, and spilling over on to the land occupied by the nuns known as the Sisters of Javouhey. The Revolutionary leader was the only person who could put a stop to the situation – otherwise the Sisters of Javouhey would have nowhere to go to pray or look after widows and children and orphans who'd been abandoned in the street by their parents, though they were still alive.

Christopher Smith adds that Cardinal Emile Biayenda and Comrade President Marien Ngouabi didn't talk about the letter that former president Alphonse Massamba-Débat sent two weeks before their meeting to ask our leader of the Congolese Revolution to step down, chop-chop, and give power back to the people, the country was in trouble. No, the cardinal was not there to ask for the restoration of the ex-president, though that's what everyone says, especially in the Congolese Party of Labour. No, the cardinal and leader of the Revolution didn't talk about that and Christopher Smith says there were witnesses that day at the headquarters: the wife of Massamba-Débat, Comrade President Marien Ngouabi's wife, his brother-in-law Mizélé, and also the captain in charge of the president's secret service, a man called Denis Ibara ...

When Christopher Smith tells us how, according to the Congolese Party of Labour, the assassination of comrade president was carried out, it's like one of those American gangster films they show at the Rex or the Duo cinema that I can't watch because they're usually for over eighteens, but fortunately they let us in if we give our pocket money to the guys on the door. Once we've seen the films in question we wonder why under eighteens aren't allowed because they don't show everything; in fact, they cover the women up too much when they are undressing and make them turn their backs to us, and the kisses are just like they're there to tell you people did it, because you never see their tongues come out and go into the other person's mouth. Well, I won't go on about that, because if I do people will say what they always say: Michel always exaggerates, and sometimes he says rude things without meaning to …

Christopher Smith explains that on 18 March at 14:10, four men in a Peugeot 404 pull up outside the headquarters of the army, which is where the residence of Comrade President Marien Ngouabi is. Because the four men are wearing military uniform everyone thinks it's normal, no reason to worry, they've come as usual for a chat with some other soldiers, they'll have a bit of a laugh, back-slap a little, talk about their wives, their mistresses, etc. So the sentries at the entrance let them go in without checking. To get to the residence of Comrade President Marien Ngouabi, you have to report to some more sentries, including agents of the president's security force, who are Cuban. That's where they check their identities closely, and all the sentries agree that it's Captain Kikadidi with three other soldiers. The Peugeot 404 now drives on towards the residence of Comrade President Marien Ngouabi, who is having lunch with his family. Captain Kikadidi and the three soldiers get out of the car and walk over to the residence. Again, it's complicated getting in, because there are two more soldiers blocking their way, one called Okamba and the other Ontsou, and like our Revolutionary leader they are northerners. But Captain Kikadidi says to Okamba and Ontsou that he's Captain Motando and he's been summoned by our comrade president in person. Okamba is suspicious because he knows what Captain Motando looks like, and he is sure that the soldier before him isn't really Captain Motando at all, as he claims. So he leaves this visitor with his colleague Ontsou and he goes over to the first guardroom to give the order for the Peugeot 404 to be removed from the compound. Meanwhile, Captain Kikadidi (claiming to be Captain Motando) is in conversation with agent Ontsou, who is actually in on the secret. He authorises Captain Kikadidi (alias Captain Motando) to go into the waiting room while someone goes to announce to Comrade President Marien Ngouabi that Captain Motando has arrived as requested.

When they tell him about his visitors, Comrade President Marien Ngouabi is surprised and says that the guy he's just seen from his dining room isn't Captain Motando, it's Captain Kikadidi, and technically Kikadidi isn't a captain any more, he's an ex-captain. Comrade President Marien Ngouabi decides to go and sort the business out himself and to go and yell at agent Ontsou, who's talking to the three unknown soldiers who came with Captain Kikadidi (alias Captain Motando). As soon as the three soldiers see the president coming towards them they get up, pretend to stand to attention, out of respect, but our Revolutionary leader notices one of them has a gun sticking out of his uniform. President Marien Ngouabi orders him to hand over his gun, but the soldier refuses. So the leader of the Revolution tries to grab it off him, and they get into a fight! As Comrade President Marien Ngouabi isn't just anybody, he quickly manages to get hold of the man's gun, using the technique they taught him at Saint-Cyr, and – Bang! Bang! – he shoots the two strangers! The one he disarmed runs off, but our president is a fine sportsman, who could beat the black Americans at running.

He gives chase, fast as a spear, and during the chase you hear shots ring out, over and over, and then over again. It's not our comrade president shooting now, it's someone else. And this someone else is Ontsou, his security agent, who is in on the secret. Ontsou has already shot his two colleagues, who were trying to help our Revolutionary leader. Meanwhile, Captain Kikadidi (alias Captain Motando) has disappeared ...

Christopher Smith is silent for a few seconds, then he repeats several times that what he has just told us is the version of the Congolese Party of Labour, who want to prove that Alphonse Massamba-Débat, the ex-president of the Republic, hatched this coup d'état, led by Captain Kikadidi, with the involvement of the presidential guard, in an attempt to get back into power, along with his fellow southerners.

The journalist then asks him what the other explanation of the assassination is. He says the other explanation, the one he believes, comes directly from the mouth of the son of the president, Marien Ngouabi Junior, and he's just about to tell us what it is ...

Marien Ngouabi Junior

Marien Ngouabi Junior is present at the actual moment his father is assassinated, so he sees it all and even tries to protect our leader of the Revolution, as he can't understand why although Okamba, his security officer, is there, he doesn't react. But Marien Ngouabi Junior is only fourteen and doesn't know how to handle a gun yet. He dreams of going to Cuba to train with Cuban soldiers and returning to Brazzaville to protect his father, the president.

Marien Ngouabi Junior has been having lunch with his father, who has been describing the physics/chemistry lesson he'd given at the university that morning. The child leaves the table before the others because it is hot and he wants to have a swim in the pool like most other children of presidents the world over. On his way over to the swimming pool he notices that people are acting oddly: Ontsou, the security officer, is standing next to someone with officer stripes, a red beret and a gun. He's not sure if this soldier is Captain Kikadidi or Captain Motando, as the Military Committee of the Party now claims, though they have no proof.

Marien Ngouabi Junior doesn't recognise Captain Kikadidi (or Captain Motando), this is the first time he's seen this guy in the compound.

He asks the three soldiers standing with the captain:

'What do you want?'

One of them answers:

'We want to see your father. It's really urgent …'

Marien Ngouabi Junior is reassured, he now thinks they are there to prepare for the celebrations of 19 March, the anniversary of an accident Comrade President Marien Ngouabi had in a helicopter. Marien Ngouabi Junior trusts agents Okamba and Ontsou, he sees them every day, he knows they ward off enemies who are trying to assassinate his dad. But the compound is too calm today, 18 March 1977. So Marien Ngouabi Junior asks Okamba and Ontsou why there are only two of them guarding his dad, when there are usually five soldiers standing here. They reply that everything's as usual, he mustn't get worked up about nothing, no one can get to Comrade President Marien Ngouabi as long as they are there to protect him, even if there are only two of them, or even only one.

Marien Ngouabi Junior turns round and sees a Peugeot 404 parked inside the compound, a short distance away. He thinks it must be part of his dad's security, which is good, because if something bad happens to the leader of the Revolution, at least the comrade president and his family can use the vehicle to make a quick getaway and hide somewhere, maybe in the French embassy.

Instead of going to the swimming pool as he'd intended, Marien Ngouabi Junior decides he'll go and play on the seesaw, and when he's been playing there for only a few minutes he hears a sound not far off, behind him, and he turns around: it's Comrade President Marien Ngouabi, fighting with the unknown soldiers he saw earlier!

Marien Ngouabi Junior shouts for help:

'Guards! Guards! Catch them!'

He runs over to the men who are fighting and on his way he bumps into one of the three unidentified soldiers who is trying to escape. Marien Ngouabi Junior may not know how to fire a revolver, but at least he can drive a car. So he gets into the car but agent Okamba comes dashing up to him:

'Junior, leave it, I'll take care of this for you …'

Marien Ngouabi Junior isn't listening, he doesn't trust anyone now, he turns on the engine, puts the car into reverse and at that moment hears: Bang! Bang! Bang! Bang!

He gets out of the car and goes back to the security post, but everyone who works at military headquarters is running away, you'd think they never got paid and it wasn't actually their job to die for Comrade President Marien Ngouabi. In their haste to get away, some of them drop their weapons on the ground, others their uniforms, so no one will know they're in the army once they're out in the street.

Marien Ngouabi Junior wants to save his dad, so he picks up an SMG. Christopher Smith swears that if you start shooting that kind of gun it's like the start of World War Three.

Marien Ngouabi Junior walks all the way round the compound with his gun in his hand. He comes to the space where he often plays football with his brothers and their friends. And there he sees three bodies lying on the ground in front of him! One of them isn't dead yet. Marien Ngouabi Junior finishes him off – Bang! Bang! Bang!

He keeps moving forward, still holding his gun. He's looking for his father, but he can't find him anywhere, even though he knows the compound like the back of his hand.

He goes back up to agent Ontsou, who's also still holding his gun, and asks him where his dad the president is.

Ontsou says:

'Your dad's over there …'

Ontsou points towards the flight of steps going up into the residence. From a distance Marien Ngouabi Junior can see a body lying near the steps. He thinks it's one of the unknown soldiers who's been shot by his father. He comes up close to the body and leans over as though to examine it. Straight away he recognises his father, who is no longer in the land of the living, though no one else in the whole country knows it yet, except for the people who assassinated him and have now vanished in the back streets of Brazzaville, some of them already drinking bottled beer in bars and celebrating their victory.

Marien Ngouabi Junior tries to lift his father's corpse, but even though Comrade President Marien Ngouabi was on the small side, he's heavy, as if there are now three or four other people inside his body.

When Marien Ngouabi Junior looks at the corpse he can't believe it's his father, the same man who was eating lunch with him less than thirty minutes ago. He leans over again: the mouth and jaw of Comrade President Marien Ngouabi are all mashed up and his teeth are all knocked out, mixed with bright red blood, the colour of the flag of the Congolese Revolution he created ...

The photo of the comrade president

Papa Roger asks me to go to Case by Case and, as usual, to buy him a bottle of red and some tobacco. The death of Comrade President Marien Ngouabi and Uncle Kimbouala-Nkaya haven't changed his routine, then.

As soon as he woke up this morning, Sunday, he went and sat out under the mango tree, and I went to join him, and we just listened to the radio, though I thought he was going to have a lot to say about yesterday's visit from Uncle René, Uncle Kinana and Uncle Moubéri. Is it because we're not meant to talk about all that when we're outside, because there are spies everywhere, like ants, who might go telling everyone we belong to the family of Uncle Kimbouala-Nkaya?

Case by Case is empty, except for me and Ma Moubobi. She's knitting a red pullover that's too small for her. It's not for her, I think, so it must be for Olivier.

The photo of Comrade President Marien Ngouabi is still there behind Ma Moubobi. It's tilted forward slightly now, and when I look up close it's as if the leader of our revolution was very sad because he knows that soon it won't be him up on the wall of the shop but another president, one of the eleven members of the Military Committee of the Party. So this is nearly the end of the road for this photo, and it doesn't want to be taken down, it would a million times rather fall off the wall by itself and not have to see itself being replaced. Ma Moubobi will also have to change her expressions, especially the name of the president when she says to the customers who promise to pay later:

'You'd better pay by the date you've promised; Comrade President Marien Ngouabi up there is my witness, he's looking at you ... Go on, take a look at him too, before I give you your goods.'

If she carries on saying that, the customers will answer:

'Who cares? Comrade President Marien Ngouabi is dead; in the future he won't be around to check if we pay or not!'

I bet she'll change the name of the president and I hope for her sake that the new name will be easy to say, because yesterday when I heard Uncle René listing all the names of the members of the Military Committee of the Party, like Joachim Yhombi-Opango or Denis Sassou-Nguesso, I noticed they were much harder to remember and pronounce than Marien Ngouabi. In fact, on the Military Committee of the Party the easiest names are Pierre Anga, Nicolas Okongo, Pascal Bima and Jean-Michel Ebaka, but none of them will ever be presidents of the Republic, not just because their names are too simple, but also because no one's frightened of them, they're only there for show, as Papa Roger says, because the most important members are Colonel Joachim Yhombi-Opango and Commander Denis Sassou-Nguesso, the president and vice-president of said Military Committee of the Party, who swore that the murderers of Comrade President Marien Ngouabi and their accomplices would be severely punished. Now from north to south and east to west, and even on the Americans' radio, everyone knows the assassins aren't a million miles away, because they've seized power and some of them are among the eleven members of the Military Committee of the Party.

'Hey you, Pauline Kengué's son! Are you listening? Still dreaming? What can I get you today? Same as usual?'

Ma Moubobi has stopped knitting and is looking straight at me. She looks like she hasn't slept since 14:30 the day before yesterday. Her eyes are like two enormous red globules, but I also have to remind myself that Maman Pauline has told me never to make fun of people's size because sometimes it's because of an illness or evil spirits who are jealous of how much money someone earns in their shop.

'Yes please, Ma Moubobi, same as usual, but nothing for Maman Pauline today ...'

She puts my father's wine and the tobacco for his nose in a bag.

'Don't lose the change!'

'I won't, Ma Moubobi!'

As I'm leaving the shop I hear her muttering behind me:

'People are so stupid, they've stopped coming to my shop because they think there's a curfew in the daytime too! How do they think I'm going to earn a living?'

Troublemakers

There are soldiers clinging to the tops and sides of the big trucks going by in long lines, with their lights on. Usually the only cars we see with their lights on in broad daylight are the hearses, when there's a burial.

I think to myself that the trucks are a kind of hearse too, especially as they're black and brand new, with red hoods. People run off at the noise coming from inside them: men, women and even children screaming in pain as the soldiers beat them, shouting orders as if they were talking to Mboua Mabé:

'Lie down! Lie down! I said lie down!'

These poor people stuffed into the trucks are referred to as 'troublemakers' or 'local lackeys of imperialism'. That's what they said in the paper today: 'troublemakers and local lackeys of imperialism will be arrested, tried and imprisoned'. But everyone can see that most of the military trucks are going towards Mont-Kamba cemetery and not towards the detention centre in Pointe-Noire. They are in completely different directions, like the back of your neck and your nose.

Sometimes the soldiers realise they've got the wrong troublemakers or the wrong local lackeys of imperialism but it's too late, they're not going to apologise, they've already beaten them about the head and stamped on their toes, and the trucks do a U-turn, drive back past the plots of these wretched people and chuck them out like sacks of potatoes then drive on looking for the real troublemakers who've been denounced by their neighbours.

There's a section of the Military Committee of the Party in every neighbourhood now. You can go and denounce trouble-makers and local lackeys of imperialism and that way earn a bit of money ...

Black cloth

Since leaving Case by Case I've seen at least twenty-five or thirty military trucks go past.

Instead of going straight home, I head down a street with no name, with the change squeezed tightly in my right hand and the bag in my left.

There's a new kind of stall everywhere: children are selling bits of black cloth in the streets, to put round your arm to show you're in mourning. Everyone's got one, and I decide I have to buy one, so I'll be OK if a military truck goes past and they notice I'm not respecting Comrade President Marien Ngouabi. The cloth in question costs twenty-five francs, the same as Papa Roger's tobacco. If I buy some my father won't be angry; in fact, he'll say it's good I haven't forgotten who I am and that I'm still a white crane of the socialist Revolution.

There are so many people selling bits of black cloth that I don't know who to buy mine from. I stop in front of someone with bare feet and a swollen belly. I feel sorry for him, his lips are so dry, I think he can't have eaten since at least 14:30 hours the day before yesterday. For him it's a bonus that Comrade President Marien Ngouabi is dead, now he can make some money, eat and maybe even buy some shoes, so he doesn't have to walk around barefoot. I have these kind thoughts, but another part of me is also wondering how he got hold of the black cloth. In any business, it's the trader who buys the goods in bulk and then sells them on, like Maman Pauline with her bunches of bananas. I quickly realise what's going on when I see some guys a few metres away from the child traders, watching them. It's the same guys who run the gangster rackets at the markets in Pointe-Noire and snatch women's bags from them on the Voungou or the Comapon bridges. They're the suppliers, the little skinny ones just do the selling and get paid a pittance, the price of a sparrow's turd. Also, because these guys see everything from where they stand, if you don't buy their stuff they'll follow you at a distance and punch you in the face as if you were an accomplice of the murderers of Comrade President Marien Ngouabi.

I hold out a twenty-five-franc coin to the boy with the bloated stomach. He looks at the coin and says:

'No, I'm not taking that!'

The hustlers are watching us; I have to be careful how I act. I speak nicely, and I smile, so the hustlers will think everything's going smoothly and we know each other really well:

'Why not? It's a nice coin; it doesn't even smell bad like the money women keep in their bras ...'

'I'm just not taking it, full stop!'

'But, brother, it's a twenty-five-franc coin; if you look closely you'll see—'

'No, I'm not taking it! I'm not your brother! This costs fifty francs now!'

He's trying to cheat me – it says on his sign on the ground that the black cloth costs twenty-five francs.

I walk away, and go over to another child, with a normal belly. He's wearing a shirt with only one sleeve, the other's gone, there are just a few shreds suggesting that it was ripped off in a fight.

I give him my twenty-five-franc piece.

'No, I'm not taking that!'

'Hey, brother, won't you take it either? Why not?'

'I'm not your brother! This costs sixty francs now!'

'But first it cost twenty-five francs, then fifty francs, and now sixty francs!'

'If you get funny with me, it'll cost a hundred – or more!'

'I'm telling you, as true as I'm Michel, son of Pauline Kengué and Kimangou Roger, I'm not buying a piece of black cloth for a hundred francs, or for more!'

'OK, I don't care; you go and tell those big guys over there, they'll sell it to you, with a few smacks in the face thrown in!'

I go back to the child with the rugby-ball belly, fifty francs is better than sixty. Turns out, he's changed his mind too, and he tells me to go and buy from his friend who got his shirt ripped in a fight. And when I turn up in front of his friend again the price has gone up to a hundred francs!

I don't want to hang around passing the time of day with them, so I buy one and carry on my way. The big guys are laughing nastily at a distance, because other people are now buying at twenty-five francs, some of them are even beating the price down, and only paying fifteen!

I tie the black cloth round my arm and tell myself Comrade President Marien Ngouabi would be pleased with me, because I paid more for it than anyone else. He'll also be pleased with me because even though everyone's saying he's well and truly dead, I think he's learning how to fly *over people's heads like the white cranes who are Russian soldiers who gave their lives on battlefields steeped in blood …*

The Mouyondzi neighbourhood

To get to the Mouyondzi neighbourhood I took the street with no name. It's not the street's fault it has no name, it's because, like most streets of its kind, it's not tarmacked, no one cares about it, it's covered in dust, and when lorries go past you have to pinch your nose and close your mouth or the dirt will go straight into your lungs and make you sick. I can't change routes or it would take me at least an hour, and once I've worked this out I'm happy because I've made up some time: it's only taken me thirty minutes to get from Ma Moubobi's shop to here.

People round here chuck their bins just anywhere, which is why the dogs in Pointe-Noire are always happy, and think of this as their turf. The first bin in front of me is a real mountain with children and dogs fighting over the rubbish, and it's not far from where my mates from school live, the Moubembés, Paul, the older one, and Placide, his younger brother. Placide is in the same class as me, and we're the same age too; we haven't had to repeat a year since primary, so we're going to make sure we don't before lycée either, and maybe before university too.

There are dogs everywhere. They're all really skinny, even though there's loads of rotten food around. I go right up to the bin too, and look closely at each of the dogs. The animals are so focused on eating, they take no notice of me.

But I've come up too close: three dogs start barking, thinking I'm going to snatch the bone they're fighting over when in fact I'm not interested in their petty quarrel. I take a step back, then another, and stand off to one side. What do I see? There, among the three mad dogs, there's one that looks exactly like Mboua Mabé. I take a step forward again, then two more, to get a better a look. My God! It's him! He's all black and skinny! It's Mboua Mabé! There's no mistaking him! I'm so happy! I want to shout three times over, like at Saint-Jean-Bosco's: Thank you, Lord! Thank you, Lord! Thank you, Lord!

I put my plastic bag down on a heap of rubbish and lunge for my dog, but the two others are barking because they think I'm going to take some of their food away.

I move forward, shouting loudly:

'Mboua Mabé! Mboua Mabé! Mboua Mabé!'

I get to less than two metres from him, and he bares his sharp teeth at me, his hair stands on end and he gets ready to leap at me as if this was the Biafran war and I was the enemy.

No! No! No! I realise at once it's not my dog, this is not Mboua Mabé. Besides, this one isn't black all over, as I thought when I saw him from a distance. He's got brown hair on each paw and is wearing a little chain round his neck.

I start running, but I can hear the dog running after me. I look behind me; he's stopped at the bag, which I forgot to pick up. He turns it this way and that with the claws of his paws, with his mouth, and rips it. He's disappointed with what he finds, and since it is impossible to eat a bottle of red wine, he attacks Papa Roger's tobacco and chews at it, as if it was a normal bone. Unfortunately for him, this tobacco is for human beings, and he starts sneezing. It's the first time I've really noticed that dogs can sneeze like us. The more he sneezes, the more other dogs come and gather round him and start barking, as if they're asking, 'What's wrong with you? Who did this to you? Tell us and we'll go and take care of him!'

I can't just head off and leave my father's wine there with these animals. If someone comes this way they will be glad to find it and have a free drink; the rule of the bin is finders keepers. So I pick up some stones and throw them at the dogs. They scatter, but return to the bag as soon as they've dodged the stone. I decide to go to Paul and Placide Moubembé's house, they'll help me. I set off running like a mad man …

When I get to the Moubembés' plot I find Placide reading a Tarzan adventure as usual, and he tells me his big brother has gone into town with their father, who's going to buy him some Salamander shoes.

I explain my problem with the dogs and he laughs:

'Are you really scared of dogs like that? Ha! Come on, I'll show you, they'll panic as soon as they set eyes on Placide Moubembé!'

We've been friends since primary school, and I like the way he sometimes shows how brave he is. Even though he's not very tall, he can leave you half dead with a punch because, as he often says himself, you don't have to be tall to be strong, just really focused at the moment you punch. He dreams of being Tarzan, but I know that's impossible, because when he tries to swing through the trees he always falls and has to put boa grease on his wounds. I have to be careful not to laugh too much when he falls, or he'll stop lending me his Tarzan adventures. Placide, too, like Tarzan, dreamed of being adopted by orangutans, who are virtually humans, and wanted to live with them. He hates the way that in most films you see at the Rex or the Duo cinema they make Tarzan talk like a wild animal, when most humans are more like wild animals than orangutans are. And anyway, the orangutans we're talking about are kind; they rescued Tarzan after the death of his parents, who were with him in the African jungle ...

So Placide and I are back at the bin now, where I was before. The dogs are still standing round Papa Roger's bottle of wine. Placide picks up a stick and approaches them. As soon as they see him coming, they drop their heads in respect and one after the other they move away.

Placide's really proud of himself. He picks up the bottle of red wine:

'Here, next time don't upset the dogs. They know me really well; they know I love animals ...'

I explain that I'm looking for Mboua Mabé, who disappeared when he heard them say on our Grundig:

Now, with its back to the wall and in its death throes, imperialism has used a suicide unit to launch a cowardly attack on the life of our dynamic leader of the Congolese Revolution, Comrade Marien Ngouabi, who died in combat with his weapon in his hand, this Friday, 18 March 1977 at 14:30 hours.

He stops me at once:

'Stop saying that! And don't say "Comrade President Marien Ngouabi" out on the street! Do you want to get arrested or what? Don't you know they even killed a captain called Kimbouala-Nkaya, from your mother's ethnic group?'

'Of course I know, Kimbouala-Nkaya was my uncle! The northerners killed him, but he turned into a white crane, and I know cranes live for ever ...'

'Ha-ha, very funny! You don't change! Kimbouala-Nkaya was your uncle?'

'I promise you! And two of my uncles that I've never met came from Brazzaville; they've run away from there and—'

'Stop! Stop!'

'Why won't you believe me when I—'

'Michel, you must think I'm stupid! If this Captain Kimbouala-Nkaya was your uncle the militia would already have arrested your parents to kill them too! You've just made it all up, as usual. Michel, you're a dreamer! You've got a problem! And all that about cranes, that's just stuff in Soviet songs we sang in primary school!'

I'm thinking: Why did I tell him about Captain Kimbouala-Nkaya being my uncle, when Uncle René asked us to be discreet?

I quickly change the subject to wipe out my stupid mistake and stop him asking too many questions about my uncle:

'Hey, Placide, you know my dog …'

'Is he one of them?'

'No, he went missing when he heard about the assassination of Comrade President Marien—'

'Don't say "Comrade President Marien Ngouabi" out on the street!'

'I mean, my dog's gone missing, I'm looking all over for him because—'

'Well, there's no point looking for him here! Dogs are like us, they stay in their own neighbourhood. If he comes here, the others will fight him and deal him a mortal blow! Go and look in your own neighbourhood, in the bins down by the River Tchinouka, for instance …'

Seeing I don't believe him, he says:

'There's some other problem weighing on you, Michel, I can tell …'

'No I'm fine, Placide, honestly …'

'No you're not, I know you!'

So I tell him the truth.

'Well, I think Papa Roger's going to yell at me: I've lost his change …'

'What? How come?'

I show him my arm.

'I took a hundred francs to buy this bit of black cloth I'm wearing, and his tobacco got eaten by one of the dogs who's scared of you …'

He takes a long hard look at me.

'When will you ever change? How much did your dad give you?'

'A five thousand Congolese franc note, all clean, and not crumpled.'

'Here then, pay me back when you can …'

'Where did you get that?'

'I sold my old Tarzan stories to the old man who runs the pavement bookshop outside the Rex cinema.'

'Oh no, I can't take that …'

'Would you rather get yelled at by Papa Roger? First you lost his tobacco and then you used his money without asking his permission, and after that you lost his change, that's a lot, Michel …'

He takes the bottle of wine from my hands.

'I'll keep it; you go and buy another one with the money I've just given you, then they'll give you the same amount of change and your father will never know. And stop going round boasting that Captain Kimbouala-Nkaya was your uncle and has turned into a white crane! It's usually troublemakers that tell lies like that, they could easily arrest your parents for it!

The dirty note

Ma Moubobi is surprised to see me come back into the shop:

'Pauline Kengué's son back again? Did I not give you back the right change?'

I tell her I forgot my father wanted two packets of tobacco and two bottles of wine.

I give her the five thousand Congolese franc note and she looks at it very uncertainly, like someone suspecting a trick:

'And why have you brought another one, when you already had the change I gave you? That would be enough to pay me with now. Besides, your father always has clean new notes!'

Without thinking I reply:

'Yes, but he gave me this one because it was too dirty and he didn't want it …'

'What? What are you saying, boy? So Roger thinks my shop is somewhere you pay with dirty money, does he?'

She tosses the bottle of wine and the packet of tobacco on to the table:

'You can tell your father that Ma Moubobi's shop isn't some rubbish bin where the dogs of Pointe-Noire all gather! And if you don't tell him, I'll come round to your house and tell him myself!'

The answer's no

Maman Pauline is out sweeping the yard. She's wearing a black scarf on her head. So she's decided to go into mourning even though Uncle René and Papa Roger don't want her to in case people ask questions in the neighbourhood and she gets into trouble when people realise we belong to the same family as Captain Kimbouala-Nkaya. On the other hand you can't actually say wearing a black headscarf is being in mourning because you really have to be in black from head to toe and shave your head completely for that. But Maman Pauline is wearing a wax wrap with pictures of little groups of birds with different coloured feathers. They're not white cranes, they're swallows, which you see everywhere – they make their nests on the roofs of the buildings at Three-Glorious-Days. I'm a bit sad the birds on my mother's wrap aren't white cranes, swallows are chatty birds, their flight isn't exactly elegant. Their droppings are always falling on people's clothes, and unless you wash them with Monganga soap the stains will never come out. Many people in Pointe-Noire think that if a swallow poops on your head it's lucky, and they go running off to play the National Congolese Lottery in the hope of winning millions. Some idiots even stand guard underneath swallows' nests waiting for them to crap on them when sometimes they don't need to go, and they're just playing among themselves, especially the children, who haven't learned how to fly and chat yet. You shouldn't go running after luck, it's just a happy accident, the only accident any of us ever wishes for …

From the way she's looking, I'm sure Maman Pauline still hasn't spoken to Papa Roger since this morning and she's in a bad mood because of the row in the night about the head shaving business. My father knows there's no point trying to make her talk; anything coming out of her mouth is going to be deadlier than viper's venom. And if she gets angry the whole day will be a write-off in this house; we might not even eat again, like last time, even if we were saved at the last minute by the terrible news of the death of Comrade President Marien Ngouabi, the arrival of Uncle René and uncles Kinana and Moubéri. When I say 'saved' that's just an expression, because there was a whole load of bad news inside that briefcase of Uncle René's …

I go and sit with Papa Roger under the mango tree. He doesn't notice I've put his bottle of wine down beside him. I listen to the Voice of the Congolese Revolution with him. On this station they always talk about the thing you're not interested in: instead of talking in depth about the death of Comrade President Marien Ngouabi and telling us something about Captain Kimbouala-Nkaya, it gives you the news from abroad. They tell you the French have just elected a new mayor of Paris, and that the man's name is Jacques Chirac. Apparently he's a fine chap, intelligent, and it's thanks to him that the current French president, Valéry Giscard d'Estaing, became president. To say thank you, this president bumped him up to prime minister in 1974. But Chirac only stayed prime minister for two years; he had plans of his own, like all intelligent people of his sort.

The Voice of the Congolese Revolution says that this

Jacques Chirac is a political magician and he can make sure the other candidates lose elections. I don't know where the journalists get this kind of top-secret stuff. They even say that when Uncle Pompidou died, three years ago, France fell into chaos. Everyone knew he was ill, but people said he would last at least till the end of his term. But no, he just went and died and they had to change presidents. Usually Pierre Messmer, Pompidou's prime minister, would have been the choice to replace Pompidou, but this Jacques Chirac, with his super intelligence, which the Voice of the Congolese Revolution has been going on about for the last thirty minutes, decided to go for Valéry Giscard d'Estaing, the Finance Minister, who really wanted to be president. So it's thanks to this Jacques Chirac that the French have now got Valéry Giscard d'Estaing as president. Hang on, though, Jacques Chirac has done lots of good things, and the French are still reaping the benefits and haven't even said thank you, says the Voice of the Congolese Revolution. Apparently, it's thanks to him that the unemployed have somewhere to go to sign up if they're looking for work, the National Employment Agency. We don't have those, though we have plenty of jobless people here as well.

As I'm listening to all this, I wonder why someone who used to be prime minister is trying to get himself elected mayor of Paris, when prime minister is a more important position than mayor of a town. I keep wondering why our national radio station gives us these good news stories and doesn't mention the name of Captain Kimbouala-Nkaya once, when he loved our country and got gunned down for no reason. Here in the Congo we're sad while the Parisians are just lazing about and feeling happy this Sunday 20 March 1977, having elected their mayor, Jacques Chirac, with no fighting, no military trucks in the streets, no telling people they have to stay home for the curfew and mustn't meet in the street in groups of more than three people between seven in the evening and seven in the morning.

Many people, like me, never knew that mayors were elected. In our country it's the president who chooses the mayors, and he orders people to go out and vote one hundred per cent or there'll be trouble. And if you get all clever and say you don't want to vote for a mayor who's been selected by the president, the soldiers who oversee the vote will put you in handcuffs and take you to a cell to be whipped with an AV42 drive chain.

'Michel, you mustn't talk to your mother if she's not speaking to you,' says Papa Roger, interrupting my thoughts.

I glance back over at my mother: she's over by the kitchen now, sweeping with her back to us. People passing in the street call out to her and she simply nods to say hello back.

'I'll drink this wine a bit later today; go and put it in the pantry.'

I take a couple of steps towards the house. At the third step, Maman Pauline sees me. She puts down her brush, comes over to me, and we both go into the living room.

'What was your father saying to you just now?'

'Er … nothing.'

'Did he mention your uncle Kimbouala-Nkaya? Tell me the truth …'

I don't know what she's driving at, so I reply:

'No, Maman, we were listening to the radio …'

'Ah! And were they talking about my brother, Captain Kimbouala-Nkaya, on the radio at last?'

'No, they were talking about Jacques Chirac …'

'Who's he, then? Was he assassinated along with your uncle?'

'He's a white Frenchman who's just been elected mayor of Paris.'

'Is that all?'

'They say he'll do anything to get someone elected president of the Republic. Also, he invented the office where people without jobs have to register to find work, the National Employment Agency and—'

'Really! As if we didn't have proper things to talk about in this country! Roger's acting very oddly at the moment!'

'He didn't say that, the Voice of the Congolese Revolution did.'

'Then it's not true, Michel! I promise you, even this Jacques Chirac doesn't exist! No one's called Jacques Chirac, that's a name they've invented so as not to talk about the murder of my brother Kimbouala-Nkaya! But we're not going to let that happen!'

She lowers her voice:

'Tomorrow your father will sleep at his first wife's, he'll leave for work early in the morning, and as soon as he's gone, you'll come with me to the Grand Marché, there's a woman who hasn't paid me for months now and—'

'The northern tradeswoman?'

'How do you know that? Did you listen to us talking last night?'

I lower my eyes.

'Look at me when I'm talking! You're taller than I am now and you're acting like you're scared! Tomorrow, when we get to the market, face to face with this northern woman, you have to pull a face like a really bad boy! I want her to be afraid of you. Try to look a bit nasty now, just so I can see if you're any good …'

I pull in my eyebrows, compress my lips and make myself

look really horrible. Maman Pauline takes a step backwards to assess the effect.

'That's sort of right, but you need to press your lips and teeth together to tighten your jaw!

I press my lips and teeth together even harder.

'That's it!'

'What if it goes wrong?'

'What? You're not frightened, are you? Would your uncle who was assassinated be frightened? When they came to his house to arrest him, I bet he got his gun out and shot, but there were too many of them; the captain couldn't shoot them all down. The woman who owes me money is called Antoinette Ebaka and—'

'She's the leader of the Congolese Revolutionary Women's Union at the market …'

'You really have been listening through the walls! I don't care if she's a member of the Congolese Revolutionary Women's Union. I want my money and I'm not going to put up with her telling me to come back next month when they've killed my brother! She has to pay me!'

There's a noise by the door and we both turn round: Papa Roger's coming in to the house.

'What's going on here, are you plotting against me?'

'I'm having a conversation with Michel! Have the Military Committee of the Party forbidden that too now, as well as killing my brother?'

Before turning on his heels, my father says:

'Pauline, don't be naïve … Watch out or you'll get our family into trouble. Antoinette Ebaka didn't kill Captain Kimbouala-Nkaya …'

Papa Roger is already on his way back out as my mother yells:

'No, but her northern brothers killed him, it's the same thing!'

Maman Pauline goes outside too, and picks up her brush again. I go back and see my father, to ask him if can go out for a few minutes.

'Is it for your mother?'

'Well, actually ...'

'Is it Mboua Mabé you want to talk to me about?'

'Um ...'

'Michel, your dog may already be dead. And besides, I'm not an idiot: you spent too long fetching my wine and tobacco, I know you took a different route to go and look for the dog. If you didn't find him then, what makes you think you'll find him this time? So the answer's no. Now don't mention that dog to me again ...'

I don't answer, but I can see he feels sorry for me.

'Listen, you can go, but talk to Pauline first, I don't want her to go on at me about it ...'

I go and stand by Maman Pauline, but she doesn't even turn round. She just says:

'I heard all that, and the answer's no.'

Ma Moubobi's rage

Ma Moubobi hasn't set foot in our house for a very long time; the last time was maybe four or five months ago, when she came round to ask Maman Pauline the name of the girl who did her braids so beautifully. My mother told her it was Célestine, the child of one of her trader friends from the Grand Marché. Célestine is the best braider in Pointe-Noire, daughters and mothers chase after her, she's so much in demand you have to book an appointment three weeks or a month ahead. But Maman Pauline doesn't have to worry about appointments because Célestine's mother, Ma Kilondo, says directly to her daughter:

'Don't keep Pauline waiting or she won't keep me the best bunches of bananas for my stall.'

So Maman Pauline only has to ask and Célestine changes all her appointments and comes and spends a whole day with us, doing my mother's hair. Maman Pauline prepares some nice food, something she really likes, spinach with palm oil and salted fish and peanut butter. In the evening she pays for her hairdo and also gives her money for a taxi. She learned from the West Africans, who are the best at complicated braids. Her fingers are really slender, and when they move they look like a spider's legs; she goes really fast, flicking about, tugging, winding, then bringing the hair together to make a knot and when it's finished, the result's amazing, it's like magic! When Célestine does a woman's braids, even if the woman has a really ugly face, she suddenly becomes beautiful, like the mermaid, Mami Wata, who lives in the rivers in our villages, with her golden hair and her fish tail. A woman who's had her hair braided properly by Célestine needn't worry: men will turn round in the street, ask her for a drink in a bar, then go somewhere private to do things I'm not going to go into here or people will say Michel always exaggerates, and sometimes he's rude without realising.

Anyway, a few months ago Ma Moubobi had the same braids done as Maman Pauline. Sadly it only lasted two days, because the poor woman was in pain and said her head hurt. She spent a night having her braids taken out by some other girls who all criticised Célestine's work and when I went into her shop I found her with an Afro big enough for a sparrow to nest in, thinking her head was a palm tree.

I'm a bit worried to see Ma Moubobi at our house, remembering how I annoyed her with my stupid explanation about my father wanting to get rid of a dirty note in her shop. So she hasn't even waited a day to come and sort out the problem. Out of respect for her, Papa Roger turns off the radio, which was tuned to the Voice of the Congolese Revolution. He was going to turn it off anyway because they still hadn't mentioned Captain Kimbouala-Nkaya; they were busy telling us that people have placed explosives in a petrol station in France. This happened in Corsica, which, according to the journalists, is an island where the people are having a difficult time because they don't want to be French any more, they want to be Corsican and they're always going on at poor President Valéry Giscard d'Estaing, the one who was elected president thanks to Jacques Chirac, who became mayor of

Paris last Sunday. Fortunately no one died as a result of the Corsicans' explosives, otherwise our radio station would have gone on and on about it, right up till the funeral of Comrade President Marien Ngouabi and in the end we'd lose track of who we were meant to be in mourning for. But this wasn't the only thing that had annoyed Papa Roger, there were other problems, again in France, in a town called Rennes, where the people generally referred to as Bretons destroyed State buildings, again by putting bombs in them – Boom! Boom! Boom! So the people responsible for this chaos are not the Corsicans because Rennes is too far from their island and there would be no point them going to plant their explosives in a place where the people generally referred to as Bretons inherited the stubbornness of their ancestors, who liked to fight all day long, a bit like Africans. But the people of Corsica and the people of Brittany are annoyed about the same things: they want their own country, they don't want to just be regions of France where they'll have to speak French, which has too many rules, and will have to ignore their own ethnic languages, which if they're not careful, as the journalists explain, will eventually disappear. The Bretons cooked up this attack, and the leaders are so pleased with what they've done they want the whole world to know about it. Which is why they put out information straight away, before other people in other regions of France steal their victory from them …

Actually, my father started to turn down the radio as soon as he realised our journalists had nothing more to say and that they'd started going on about all the bad things that happened yesterday, especially what happened to our brothers in Comrade President Nicolae Ceauşescu's Romania. According to the Voice of the Congolese Revolution, we now know how many people died there two weeks ago in an earthquake.

There were more than one thousand five hundred dead, not forgetting the eleven thousand injured and the thousands of people who now have nowhere to sleep.

I can see from Ma Moubobi's face she's not very pleased and that I'm going to get into trouble today. She doesn't say hello to Papa Roger, she sits down where I was sitting before, because I have to give my place to her, out of politeness.

Looking around, left to right, she asks my father:

'Where's Pauline?'

My father's head sweeps from left and right too, as if Maman Pauline's hiding somewhere.

'I expect she's in the kitchen. Do you want me to call her?'

Ma Moubobi turns to me:

'Michel, you go and call her, not your father! I can tell from your manners you're a spoiled only child!'

I trail off towards the kitchen, and peer in the door, without entering: but my mother's not there. I'm in the house now, and since I can't find Maman Pauline in the living room, I go into their bedroom: she's there, weeping in a corner, with a lighted candle and an old photo of Captain Kimbouala-Nkaya. From where I'm standing I can see the picture clearly, thanks to the light of the candle. My uncle is wearing his military uniform, but not his combat gear, soldiers never go into battle wearing a tie, war isn't about showing the enemy you're better dressed than them. The captain is wearing a white shirt, gloves as white as the shirt, stripes on his shoulders and badges everywhere, on either side of his chest. His head is turned to the right a bit like in the photo of Comrade President Marien Ngouabi where his eyes are also turned to the right, but unlike our leader of the Revolution, who's wearing a cap, the captain is bareheaded, he has short hair, a little moustache and is smiling as though someone was distracting him while the photo was being taken. Maman Pauline must have taken this photo out of the case where she hides her really expensive wax wrappers, her jewellery, important documents like her birth certificate, papers that prove she is the owner of our plot, identity papers and my school reports, going back to primary school.

My heart is beating really loudly, because I'm so upset to see her in this state, so Maman Pauline hears me breathing and turns round:

'What are you doing here? Can't you see I'm busy? Why didn't you knock first?'

I explain that Ma Moubobi is outside and wants to see her straight away.

'She wants to see *me* straight away? If she wants me to call Célestine to come and do her braids, you can tell her I'm sleeping and I'll stop by and see her at the shop!'

'OK, I'll tell her that ...'

I take one step, then another, but she stops me:

'No, wait, I will see her ...'

When we get to the living room she stops, looks in the mirror above the wardrobe, licks her fingers and wipes away the signs of her tears. She tightens her wrapper around her waist, adjusts her top and the black scarf covering her head.

We come out of the house, me in front, my mother behind ...

'Pauline, I shut up shop in a hurry to come over and see you and, as I was telling Roger, a customer has just told me that this famous captain who was murdered yesterday in Brazza-ville was your brother ... Is it true? Is that why you're wearing a black scarf, Pauline?'

My mother glances first at my father, who drops his gaze. Then she looks over at me, and I do the same. She answers:

'No, he's not my brother ...'

Papa Roger and I lift our heads and look straight at Maman Pauline. She looks away.

But Ma Moubobi doesn't stop there:

'So what I heard earlier isn't true?'

'Don't listen to people, they'll tell you all sorts of different things, just to make trouble ...'

Ma Moubobi is pleased to hear this, but since she still looks unconvinced, Maman Pauline changes the subject to really confuse her.

'How's our little Olivier Moubobi? How is he getting on learning to be a bus conductor?'

As soon as anyone mentions her son, Ma Moubobi turns into a different person, all happiness, and giving you free stuff from her shop. 'Oh, my darling little Olivier? How kind of you to think of him, Pauline ... Such an intelligent boy! He's bringing in lots of money for his boss; next month he's being put in charge of all the bus conductors who work for him. And that's not all: he even has a girlfriend!'

'Well, that's good news!'

'Isn't it just, Pauline! I'm saved ... OK, she's a bit thin, I don't like that, but my son's made a good choice! He's done very well for himself!'

'How do you mean?'

'Well, Rosalie, who may be my daughter-in-law one day, is not just anyone ...'

'So you've met this Rosalie's parents?'

'I have! She doesn't have a father, which is always better; Olivier's father bunked off too. *But*, wait for it Pauline, Rosalie's mother is an extraordinary woman, you know her, she's called Antoinette Ebaka, she's the leader of the Grand Marché section of the Revolutionary Union of Congolese Women.'

My mother, my father and I all look at each other. Once

again, Maman Pauline acts like she's just calmly speaking the truth:

'No, I don't know her ...'

'She sells bananas at the Grand Marché; you can't not know her, you know all the traders, and all the traders know you! She's spoken to me about you before and—'

'I'm telling, you, I don't know her! She must buy her bananas from someone else ...'

'Really? Oh well, never mind, if she drops into my shop one of these days I'll bring her over to introduce her to you!'

'Why not, Ma Moubobi?'

'I swear you really have to meet her! Besides, she has another daughter, called Elika, she's Rosalie's twin, so your little Michel could see if—'

'Michel needs to get into Karl Marx Lycée before he thinks about that kind of thing. He needs to finish his studies and, God willing, go to Europe, to take them further. Young people today start early with women, and if you're not careful they drop their studies, have children and become gangsters down at the market ...'

Ma Moubobi looks put out. She thinks Maman Pauline is talking about Olivier:

'Hang on, Pauline, it sounds like you're getting at me there! Are you trying to say it was Olivier's choice to give up his studies? It was the other pupils who upset him! Besides, Olivier has a job, and a good job! Do you think most of the young people who go to Three-Glorious-Days or the Karl Marx Lycée find work in this country?'

Papa Roger intervenes:

'Ma Moubobi, Pauline wasn't saying that to get at you, she's talking generally. I mean, what she was trying to say was—'

'Roger, am I talking to you or your wife? I'm no fool. I

know when I'm being got at in secret, and that's what Pauline's just done! And another thing – explain to me why, when you want to get rid of a five-thousand-franc note, you give it to your child so he'll come and buy the same thing twice at my shop. That's an insult to me, Roger! You wouldn't do that in some white person's shop in the town centre! So you think my shop is somewhere you can pay with a dirty note, do you?'

Papa Roger is surprised:

'Hold on, what's all this about a dirty note?'

Maman Pauline is surprised too:

'A dirty note? What are you talking about? You're picking a fight with us over nothing!'

Ma Moubobi points her finger at me:

'I'm telling you, your boy came into my shop today with a very dirty note, he said you'd given it to him to spend in my shop, Roger, because it was too dirty and you didn't want it!'

Papa Roger calms her down:

'Ma Moubobi, we'll sort that out with him. I clearly remember giving him a clean note.'

Ma Moubobi rummages in her bra and takes out a note:

'Here's the dirty note in question, I've kept it! Look how dirty it is! I'm going to give it back to you, I'm not keeping this stinky thing in my shop, it will bring me bad luck!'

Maman Pauline's not having that:

'Listen, Ma Moubobi, if that's why you've come round here, you can just go straight back to your shop!'

'You're turning me out now, are you?'

'Yes, I'm turning you out. First you come round talking about my brother who's been murdered, I mean this captain I don't know who's been murdered, and now it's some story about a dirty banknote! Even if it is dirty, does that mean what you buy with it is dirty too? If it's dirty, why did you put it in your bra?'

'I'm leaving!'

She throws the dirty banknote on the ground and makes for the exit, where we hear her yelling:

'My shop is not a rubbish bin! I don't want any of you to set foot in it ever again! Pathetic people!'

The moment Ma Moubobi's out of sight, Maman Pauline and Papa Roger start attacking me. Too many questions, and I can't wriggle my way out.

'Is this story about the banknote true?' Maman Pauline asks me.

'If it is true, my boy, you're in big trouble; you'll have to go and apologise by yourself!' my father says.

'Answer me!' orders Maman Pauline.

'Yes, answer us!' Papa Roger shouts.

I wait a few seconds, and then I say: 'No, it's not true ...'

The cardinal's cousin

It's maybe midnight or one in the morning. From my bed I can hear dogs barking far off. Is Mboua Mabé with them? Is he happy, surrounded by his friends, who are more important than me, though if it hadn't been for me he'd have still been a wretched animal no one wanted to buy at the Grand Marché, even half price? If he thinks he's better off where he is then I'm going to stop looking for him, and I don't care if he's in Voungou, by the River Tchinouka or down at the bins in the Mouyondzi. It's over anyway, neither Papa Roger nor Maman Pauline want him back. I bet he's picked up some bad habits since he's been wherever he is, things I never wanted him to do with she-dogs and that I can't go into here or people will think Michel always exaggerates and sometimes he says rude things without meaning to. But in my heart I am actually the kind of boy who doesn't keep his anger in the fridge and heat it up later, so I forgive my dog his bad behaviour and because of that he'll turn into a crane and protect Comrade President Marien Ngouabi, because it's no coincidence that he vanished as soon as he heard the terrible news, news that no other dog in the whole country was capable of hearing.

During the meal, after Ma Moubobi had left our place in a temper, I didn't have much appetite left once Maman Pauline had said she wasn't hungry, she couldn't eat as her brother's corpse was still not buried and she'd never know where it lay. Also, she brought us our food under the mango tree without once shouting that she wasn't our slave. I was amazed by this pleasant behaviour given that she's stopped talking much and spends most of her time in the bedroom, sobbing, praying as if our house was the mosque the Moslems go to at the Grand Marché.

Papa Roger and I ate in silence. The bits of porcupine meat weren't as tasty as before, and it wasn't Maman Pauline's fault, the dish was well made, but it's hard to enjoy your food when your heart's aching. You don't just taste food with your mouth, your whole body is involved, but my body and Papa Roger's body weren't concentrating on what we were eating, so we were just eating to get something down into our stomachs.

Later, after dark, Papa Roger listened to the evening news on the radio. They still hadn't said anything about the captain's death and I came in to pour him a glass of wine just at the moment when our journalists were congratulating the French rugby team on their victory over Ireland in the Five Nations Cup in Dublin, 15–6 …

Maman Pauline had already shut herself up in the bedroom, turned out the light and begun weeping for Captain Kimbouala-Nkaya again. The noise of military trucks passing in the street made my heart pound. I wondered what they could be transporting at this hour of night. They were heading for Mont-Kamba cemetery, like in the daytime, except there were no people inside them weeping. They had the streets and avenues all to themselves; no one dared go out, not even a cat. Our town had never been so silent, as if something even bigger, even more serious, was about to happen. But what could be bigger or more serious than the death of Comrade

President Marien Ngouabi, and, for our family, the death of Captain Kimbouala-Nkaya? Maybe if you add up little things and put them together with some other little things it will make big things happen? Papa Roger had told me, for example, that in the late afternoon the militia had arrested François Nzitoukoulou, a man who works at the Atlantic Palace Hotel and who he knows well because they both work on reception. Sometimes if there's a problem with rooms, they call each other to sort it out: my father puts up his client for a night, then François Nzitoukoulou takes him back for the next night, and the other way round when my father gets stuck at the Victory Palace. According to my father, François Nzitoukoulou has been arrested because he's said to be a cousin of Cardinal Emile Biayenda. His neighbours had gone to the Public Order Offices that the Military Committee of the Party set up in each neighbourhood this morning. The State gives lots of money to true patriots who catch the enemies of the Revolution, my father explained. Now Cardinal Emile Biayenda had been at the headquarters a few hours before the assassination of Comrade President Marien Ngouabi.

I asked my father:

'Did you know he was the cousin of Cardinal Emile Biayenda, even though they didn't have the same name?'

'Yes, I had the honour of putting the cardinal up at the Victory Palace; François himself asked me, as a favour to his cousin. Our suites are better than the ones at the Atlantic Palace ...'

Sweet dreams

It upsets me to hear Maman Pauline weeping like that in their bedroom in the middle of the night. I bet she's looking at the photo of Uncle Kimbouala-Nkaya.

Papa Roger tries to comfort her:

'Pauline, have you seen what time it is? I understand your pain, but this is out of all proportion. If you carry on like this—'

'Carry on how? Watch what you say!'

My mother tells Papa Roger off really loudly, and I can hear everything, as if I was standing outside their bedroom door:

'Let me be, Roger! Wouldn't you rather go and sleep at Martine's? What are you doing here in my bed anyway? Your head's not here! Leave me to weep for my brother and don't touch me, or I'll go and sleep in Michel's room!'

I put my hands over my ears so I can't hear them, but it's stupid, because suddenly I can hear my own heart beating, and it's beating so loud that I feel like I want to sick it up, so I can breathe. I need to think of something different, something happier, or keep myself busy with something like reading till I fall asleep.

I open the book I brought home from school last Thursday. The title is *Understanding the Geography of the Congo*. They say in this book that the area of the Congo is only 342,000 square kilometres and that there aren't as many of us as there are Zairians, there are over twenty-four million of them and fewer than two million of us but we have as many problems as the twenty-four million Zairians. It also says that our country only has two seasons: the rainy season and the dry season. Now if I'm not mistaken, this book has got it wrong because we don't have two seasons, we have four! From October to December it's the long rainy season and it's very hot: that's the first season. The short dry season starts in January and ends in February: this is the second season, when there's hardly any rain and it's too hot. The rainfall in this season isn't nearly as heavy as in the season before. From March to April you get the short rainy season, when it rains, but not all the time like in the long rainy season: this is the third season. And lastly there's the fourth season, between May and September, the dry season, when it hardly rains at all and sometimes you have to wear a jumper.

Understanding the Geography of the Congo isn't even a real book, it's just a bundle of photocopied pages held together with a bit of wire at the top and another at the bottom. You can't tell who wrote it, there's no name on it. At the bottom of the first page, in red, it says, *It is strictly forbidden to steal these pages. Parents of miscreants will be summoned.* You might mistake this for the title of the book, when in fact it's just to scare pupils off tearing the pages out and taking them home. They do this because they think the teacher will pick the homework questions out of here. So they study them like parrots, and if the question's different the parrots are lost. Some people pinch the pages so they can cheat in exams. It's like the parrots, because you need a question that's got the answer on the page you've stolen. I'm not like either of these types of miscreants. During the geography lesson, the teacher asks us to get into groups of five or six and he picks the most intelligent pupil in each group and lets them take the text-book home. At the weekend this pupil has the others round to their house to prepare the presentation. We do a presenta-tion every Monday, which means we talk in class in front of the teacher and the girls, who pull faces, and the boys who pretend to be gorillas and scratch their backs. If you take too much notice of these comedians, you'll lose your thread and start saying things that aren't in *Understanding the Geography of the Congo.*

Normally, if it hadn't been for the terrible news of the death of Comrade President Marien Ngouabi, my three class-mates would have been round that afternoon to prepare the presentation with me. That's right, Etienne Tokoutani-Lelo, Zéphirin Malanda-Ngombé and Louise Mwana-Watoma would have been round here. A week before chaos broke out in our country, I was sitting with them right where Papa Roger is now, listening to his Grundig. We sat in a circle so we could all see each other. As usual, I was holding *Understanding the Geography of the Congo* and it was also me asking questions to make sure we'd understood everything. Then we each had to recite in turn what it said about the different peoples, the Vilis, the Yombés, the Larsi, the Kunsi, the Mbochis, the Tékés, etc. It was really long, so I asked Louise to take the book and ask the questions instead. In any case, Etienne and Zéphi-rin won't be the teacher; they don't want to look silly in front of Louise. And there's another thing: we all wanted Louise to take over from me because she's really nicely dressed, in a grown-up see-through clingy dress. Louise is already one of those women men turn round to look at in the street. She gets whistled at, the black capitalists stop in their cars, she has to explain that she's a minor, she lives with her mum and dad, who might go and tell the police if they force her to get in the car and take her to a place she doesn't know and make her do things I'm not going to go into here, or people will say Michel always exaggerates, and sometimes he says rude things without meaning to. Anyway, Louise is almost a real woman. She wears ladies' heels, lipstick, jewellery, which all belong to her mother, Ma Longonia, who was Miss Pointe-Noire before our parents even knew we were going to be born and that Comrade President Marien Ngouabi was going to come to power and be assassinated on 18 March 1977 at 14:30. Louise has already told us that back then the rich people in this town all wanted to go out with Ma Longonia and some of them promised her all the gold in the world! While she was telling us all this, I was wondering if it's a good idea, when you're chatting up a woman, to promise her all the gold in the world. What if the woman leaves you, or gives all your money to the other men she loves in secret, younger, better looking men with more muscles, what do you do then, when you're left with nothing? Louise did us an imitation of her father's voice the day he tricked her mother into marrying him:

'My dad said to my mum: "Miss Pointe-Noire, you are all the gold in the world to me, and when I'm with you I feel like gold too, I shine …"'

We couldn't really see what was so great about this, but Louise added:

'My mum had never heard a man say that before, so she married my father straight off, and I'm their only child … I mean, I know my dad's twenty-five years older than my mum, but he's a great guy.'

At this point Zéphirin started laughing:

'So did he end up giving all the gold he had to Ma Longonia?'

Now Etienne started teasing her:

'Oh! Oh! Oh! Give me a bit of gold, and I can have a nice big bracelet made!'

Louise didn't realise they were joking, and she got cross:

'You're not men yet! You don't realise, that's what chatting up is! You don't get it – that was my dad's way of telling my mother he would love her even after they were both dead? Honestly, *mmcht*!' She smacked her lips disdainfully.

What really turns us on about Louise is her amazing hairstyles, though it's not Célestine who does her braids, it's her own mother. And what really gets to Louise is when Etienne, Zéphirin and I look too hard at her chest. Which is why, as soon as I asked her to take my place asking the questions, she used the textbook to hide her chest.

Etienne and Zéphirin are always competing to get Louise to fall in love with them. That's why they're always distracted while we're working. They tell funny stories, thinking Louise is going to fall for that, but they end up laughing at their own stupid jokes about disabled people running races and getting overtaken at the last moment by an old snail who set off last.

I know Louise is secretly in love with me. My cousin Gilbert Moukila, who all women just adore, taught me things about how you get a woman to fall fatally in love with you. Etienne and Zéphirin don't know, and I'm not going to tell them the secret, or one of them will capture Louise's heart and kick it around like a football. Gilbert Moukila, who we also call 'Magician', says that for women love steals up unseen, and even if you see it come racing up like a sports car, you have to stay calm, chill out, pretend you haven't noticed, or love will spread its wings and fly away and go and find a home with the kid who always stayed calm. Magician's right, and that's why I stay calm too, and wait in my corner for love to come along in its own time. Last month, though, I did lose my cool a bit, I wrote a poem and showed it to Louise, without telling Etienne and Zéphirin. I haven't finished it yet, there are still only four lines and I keep altering them because I feel like it's still too long, with too many syllables, when what I'd like to write is alexandrines like the poetry in our French books. Here are my four lines, it's only a draft, I still might change it tomorrow, or the day after:

White cranes will envy all your dresses,
Spotless they'll be, for all eternity
I'll wash them every night while you are sleeping.
And fresh each morning each of them will be.

When Louise read this she looked me up and down, the way you look at people who are badly dressed and dare go walking about in the centre of town, you'd think they had no sense of shame.

'Michel, did you copy this out of somewhere?'

I thought to myself: If she thinks I've copied it she must have really liked my little poem, it must be good.

Feeling very proud I replied:

'Do you really think I would copy something?'

'Well, who did you write it for? Because if you look carefully, it doesn't mention the girl's name!'

Maybe at this point I should have declared my feelings. Instead of announcing that I'd written the poem for her, I said:

'It's for the girl who will one day be my wife, who I'll love from dawn to dusk …'

We'd moved away from the mango tree a bit because Etienne and Zéphirin wanted to know what we were talking about and why Louise was listening to me with that friendly, smiling expression.

But when she read it for the second time, then again a third time, she didn't look so friendly.

'Tell me the truth, Michel, you wrote that for Caroline, your girlfriend in primary school, Lounès's sister …'

'No, Caroline was in love with my enemy Mabélé, not with me …'

'So it's really over between you and her?'

'Yes, it's better that way, she messed around, it made me unhappy. Anyway, I don't speak to her brother any more, and Caroline doesn't live in Pointe-Noire now, her parents sent her to Brazzaville because she was getting too involved round here with boys who were too old for her …'

Louise was really happy now:

'So you mean that right now you don't have a girlfriend, right?'

I blew my chance again, maybe because I didn't want her to tease me and say I was a cold shoulder, meaning someone who never manages to get a girl.

'Think I'm a cold shoulder, do you? Well, I'm not actually, I do have a girlfriend!'

'Really? Is she in school with us? Do I know her?'

'No, she doesn't go to our school, you don't know her.'

'So what's her name?'

'I'm not telling you her name because she wants it to stay top secret between her and me or our love will fly away and make its home with another boy who's calm and chilled …'

She started patting her hair and touching up her lipstick in front of me. It didn't even seem to bother her or annoy her that my eyes were glued to her top half, which is so round and curvy, if you're not careful you might actually think she's got two giant papayas hidden in there. There she was, getting more beautiful by the second, and Etienne and Zéphirin were starting to sulk over there, and I just couldn't think what to say to her. Magician often says that if you don't know what to say when you're with a girl, it's better to say nothing than risk spoiling everything by letting your mouth open and say any old thing before it's asked your head for permission. If you say nothing, the silence will speak for you.

'You see, Michel, I'd like a boy to write that to me. The girl in your poem's really lucky ...'

'In what way, lucky?'

'Well, you wrote it in your poem: she won't have to wash her dresses, you'll do it for her ...'

I wanted to tell her she was the girl in my poem, but on the other hand I thought that if she took it badly I'd be embarrassed in front of Etienne and Zéphirin, who were already fighting over her and would go round telling everyone in school. I said nothing, she went back to our two friends, we all said goodbye, and they left.

I stayed outside our plot watching how Louise walked and how her Netherlands wiggled. I put my hand on my chest: my heart was racing.

So I was in love, and I knew that I'd stay in love, despite all the bad news about the assassination of Comrade President Marien Ngouabi and Captain Kimbouala-Nkaya, which meant I wouldn't see her again this week because school would be closed until after the funeral for the leader of our revolution.

Often when we're preparing our geography presentation under the mango tree, we find we don't understand what it says in the manual, and Papa Roger has to come and help us. He turns the pages quickly and is amazed at what's in there, because they didn't teach it like that in his day:

'What's this nonsense? How can they say, "The Congo is a country that straddles the equator"? First they need to explain what the equator is!'

At this point he turns into a geography teacher himself. He tells us that the equator is something you can't see, it's an invisible line that runs all the way round the earth a bit like when you wear a belt so your trousers don't fall down in front of people, except the equator isn't there to stop the Earth falling, just to separate the people in the north from the people in the south. And he adds that the world wasn't divided up properly, because the people in the south suffer so much more than the people in the north.

One day I showed my friends the map of the world in our textbook:

'We're lucky – our Congo is one of the eleven countries the equator goes through, along with six African countries: Somalia, Zaire, Sao Tomé et Principe, Uganda, Kenya and Gabon …'

Zéphirin pulled a sad face.

'What about the countries it doesn't go through, what will happen to them?'

I closed the textbook, because it was the end of our session, and I replied:

'What do we care if the equator doesn't go through them? We didn't decide it should exist in the first place, or that our country should be astride it. That's their hard luck, that's why they call them "non-aligned".'

I don't want to read the textbook now. Usually I do, telling myself that the next day I'll go into class and what I've revised will be fresh in my mind, so that when the teacher asks a question I'll put my hand up faster than the others, to show them that Michel's a hard worker, he doesn't copy the stupid things the people next to him are writing.

If there hadn't been all this toil and trouble I'd have left the house tomorrow morning at six o'clock to go to school. When I get to Three-Glorious-Days there are people everywhere, scooters, push bikes, groups of people who've walked for hours from neighbourhoods like Mbota or Fond Tié-Tié. They're already sweating even though the sun hasn't come out yet. They're wearing sandals, with the school uniform, which is compulsory: the boys all in beige, girls in dark blue trousers and a light blue shirt. They're all talking. They say rude things about the headmaster, the monitors, the teacher who's always asking the girls round to his house even though they're pupils and their breasts aren't fully developed yet. We can't stay outside all morning, suddenly the bell will sound, which is the sign to stop chatting and go into class. I'm in there somewhere, too; I've walked to school from our neighbourhood, Voungou, because Maman Pauline says only the children of black capitalists demand to be driven to school.

'Michel, imagine if God gave the lame back their legs, would they be asking to be driven around? No, they'd want to walk! So thank the Almighty for your legs. He'd be disappointed if you didn't use them!'

When I get to school, first I buy some doughnuts from the old Beninese lady, Mama Couao, who sells them very cheap to schoolchildren. I also buy some corn soup with the pocket money Maman Pauline or Papa Roger has given me. I sit down on the bricks lying here and there and eat as if there was no tomorrow. If Zéphirin comes up I'll give him a bit because his parents often punish him by taking away his pocket money because he wouldn't do the washing-up or got bad marks. After we've had our quick snack, I go into the big yard, walk across and enter an old three-storey building on the other side with a roof made of rusted sheet metal. The first years' classroom is in this building, on the ground floor; the second years' is on the first floor; the third years' is on the second floor and the fourth years' is on the top floor. So you can see who's had to repeat a year because they stay on the same floor, and you can easily see who's clever because each year they go up a floor. Once you get to the class on the top floor, the fourth year, you've won, because the Karl Marx Lycée is within reach, and one day I'll go to that school, it's by the sea, and I'll like that, because I can watch the white cranes flying *above us, moaning as they go.*

In the classroom I sit in the row by the wall, next to the window. I sit down at the front desk with Albert Makaya, the son of the headmaster of the school. Louise is behind us, with Etienne and Zéphirin. Through the window I can see everything that's going on outside. As soon as the birds come and sit in the flame tree in the middle of the yard, I turn my head without thinking. I forget I'm in class, that Monsieur Yoka, our geography teacher, is reciting the complicated names of all our rivers, like the Likouala-Mossaka, the Sangha, the Loufoulakari, the Loudima, the Louessé, etc. It was Monsieur Yoka talking about the rivers that made me drift off even further while I was listening to the birds. I see forests, grasslands, animals of every shape and size. I see the smoke rising off bush fires. I see peasants returning from the fields with sacks filled with yams and roots. It's tough, their village is up high; they have to climb the hill carrying many kilos on their heads. And I write that in my exercise book, scribbling away, I'm afraid if I don't write them down, these beautiful things will vanish like smoke, and I'll forget them. I write about how the smoke meets the sky, but the wind blows the smoke away and the sky turns blue again, and I'm running, Michel is running, and I get to a clearing where Louise is waiting for me in a long white dress, with bluebirds circling her head.

I jump as Monsieur Yoka raps his metal ruler on my desk.

'Michel, you're dreaming again!'

Everyone laughs, but they won't laugh when Monsieur Yoka asks a difficult question and I raise my little hand to give the correct answer and the teacher congratulates me:

'Well done, daydreamer!'

Unfortunately, just as I start feeling proud, he adds:

'Tell me, Michel, which little bird whispered the right answer in your ear?'

At this everyone laughs, from the front of the class to the back, even though it was me who smoothly recited that the River Louessé is a large tributary of the Niari with a basin of almost 16,000 square kilometres! They're all laughing, but do they really get what that means? No. I don't understand what I've just recited either, but because I said exactly what it said in the book I revised from at the weekend, Monsieur Yoka can't contradict me, he has no choice but to say well done, then to cancel out the 'well done' by calling me a daydreamer ...

Louise sometimes slips me little notes complimenting me. I never turn around because Etienne and Zéphirin keep an eye on everything, and they're the first to laugh when I get called a daydreamer. In the end, though, it's me Monsieur Yoka asks to be the leader when we prepare the presentation for next week. So, the teacher recognises that though I dream about birds, I can still produce the right answers, that they've been biding their time in my brain till the moment I wake them up and decide how to use them and generally show some intelligence.

I don't care if the pupils now call me 'daydreamer' in the school yard. They don't know that one of Louise's congratulatory notes said, in her beautiful handwriting: *My dream boy*. She'd drawn two hearts, with a line through them. Which meant that when you're in love, both hearts are astride the equator, which explains why people who can't sit astride a horse fall off and hurt themselves …

Monday 21 March 1977

La Chine en colère

'Michel, wake up!'

I rub my eyes, because I'm seeing Maman Pauline double, I might almost be dreaming.

I've slept in my clothes. I don't know exactly when I fell asleep. Oh no, I do, actually, it was while I was thinking about the little pieces of paper Louise passes me under the desk in class to congratulate me when the others call me daydreamer.

I get out of bed and say to my mother:

'I have to get washed first because—'

'No, we mustn't be late! Use the wash bag I gave you, there's a flannel in there, you'll be quicker.'

I go outside with a plastic cup full of water and the wash bag my mother bought me at Printania. Inside there's a red toothbrush, some Diamond Enamel toothpaste, some Palm-olive soap and some cotton buds.

I bet Maman Pauline came running into my room as soon as Papa Roger left the house, already wearing his work clothes for the Victory Palace Hotel, even though he could easily get changed there. He puts on his uniform before he leaves to show off. I don't blame him, it's a great uniform: a well-ironed white shirt, a black tie, a jacket and some brown trousers, black braids on the shoulders of the jacket and a fine cap, like the ones worn by the naval captains you see at the port in Pointe-Noire.

By my reckoning my father left the house around five thirty or six o'clock in the morning. Maman Pauline came into my room about thirty minutes later. She waited that long just in case Papa Roger came back because he'd forgotten his wallet or the keys to the house where Maman Martine lives, where he'll sleep this evening with my brothers and sisters who wouldn't be my brothers and sisters if we were European because we're not blood relations and Papa Roger already had a family when he started chatting up Maman Pauline to get her to be his second wife. I've already mentioned that I often go to see Maman Martine too, in the Joli-Soir neighbourhood, and she treats me like one of her own children, as though I'd come out of her belly too. She knows how much I love little Maximilien and little Félicienne, who peed all over me. She also knows that Marius and I talk a lot because we're the same age. When I talk to my little sister Mbombie she keeps a careful eye on me. Ginette is my favourite sister; Georgette, my baby sister, is a bit bossy with me, but it's just her way of showing she loves me. When I'm at their house I always sleep in Yaya Gaston's studio, he's the oldest ...

So now I'm relieving myself in the toilet, which isn't a real toilet, just four bits of sheet metal put together so that nosy people can't see the shape of us naked from out in the street and make fun of us.

I brush my teeth, then I quickly use the flannel that I've poured the rest of the water in my cup on to. I scrub under my armpits and also in the parts I won't go into detail about here or people will say oh, Michel, he always exaggerates, sometimes he says rude things without meaning to.

I can already hear Maman Pauline calling me, saying it will be my fault if we're late.

'Get dressed quickly, and come into the living room, I need your help with something ...'

What does she want me to do for her before we leave? I rack my brains, I can't think. I stop and think some more. I pick out a pair of trousers and a wax-print shirt with a repeating pattern of Marien Ngouabi's face printed on it. No one can say I don't love the leader of our revolution. I remember to tie the bit of black cloth round my arm; after all, I paid a hundred francs to the child criminals who exploit the death of presidents to get rich themselves. Someone would have to be really mean to say anything to me when I'm wearing this outfit, with my bit of black cloth, because when you think about it, even if someone who's jealous of me saw me, they'd understand that I'm the boy in deepest mourning in the whole of Pointe-Noire, maybe in the whole of the Congo.

It's the first time I've been out in these shoes, the ones the kids at school call *La Chine en colère* – 'angry Chinas'. I'd nagged Papa Roger over and over to get him to buy them for me, because everyone was talking about them, and everyone had a pair. When my dad saw me taking them out of the box he shouted:

'Are those *Angry Chinas?*'

He told me off, saying it was ridiculous to walk around in things like that. They look like the kind of shoes you'd wear in a retirement home for whites, and even white people would never wear something like that.

'They looking like dancing shoes! Are you doing ballet, then?'

I disagree, because at school if you don't have a pair of *Angry Chinas* they treat you like some country bumpkin, an idiot who doesn't know how to dress like those swashbuckling types who go off to Paris and come back to the Congo in the long dry season and impress the girls. A craze for these shoes hit our country after everyone saw the film *Enter the Dragon,* where Bruce Lee wore *Angry Chinas,* white socks and a black-and-white kung fu uniform. Everyone in all the cinemas of Pointe-Noire cheered, everyone knew Bruce Lee would win in the end, because of his *Angry Chinas,* his feet moved so fast, if you blinked for just a second you might miss the moment when he throws a kick at the baddy, called O'Hara, who's twice his size. O'Hara was a serious guy; with one blow he could split a brick. Even though he was smaller, Bruce Lee fended off all his attacks. Thanks to his *Angry Chinas* he could leap really high in the air with one leg out in front to kick his opponent and the other forming a triangle, to give him strength.

The gangsters of Pointe-Noire all buy *Angry Chinas* now, they're good for fighting in and also for running away when you're being chased by the police. My *Angry Chinas* are black like the ones Bruce Lee wore in *Enter the Dragon,* but I'm not going to wear them with white socks because at school the thing to wear is no socks and short trousers, to show your ankles. So I hitch up my trousers and copy the way Bruce Lee uses his legs. I feel really light, as though I've nothing on my feet. I love the way it works in real life as well as in films, even here in Pointe-Noire.

I come out of my room, intending to impress Maman Pauline, but in fact it's the other way around, and she really scares me: she's sitting there in the middle of the living room, with her back to me, with a wrapper covering her whole body. All I can see is her head, and she's taken off the headscarf she wore for mourning.

'Come over here,' she says.

On the table is her handbag, and next to it, a bar of soap, some scissors and a packet of Gillette razor blades.

'Shave my head ...'

I start to get worried now. I love her hair, and I don't want her to spoil it. Besides, she's still got the braids that Célestine did for her not long ago. Usually they last for a couple of months, not a couple of weeks, before you undo them and do something different.

I can't disobey Maman Pauline this early in the morning, or the whole day will go up in smoke, like a bushfire, starting in our living room and spreading till it reaches a ghastly climax at the Grand Marché, where she'll yell at me in front of all the traders and customers.

I go behind her, careful not to knock over the bucket of water next to her.

'What do I have to do, *Maman*?'

'It's easy: first you cut the braids with the scissors, then you put on the foam, then you get a Gillette razor to shave it cleanly, like when Roger shaves his beard. Careful not to cut me!'

I'm still hesitating, because I think maybe she'll change her mind when she thinks about how ugly she'll look with her bare skull showing.

'What are you waiting for, Michel? Do you want to make us late? Come on, hurry up, stop daydreaming!'

I pick up the scissors and go, Chop! Chop! Chop!

Her hair falls all around her. I start to get the hang of it as I go. I do her whole head in under five minutes.

Maman Pauline runs her hand over it.

'Good! Now wet my head and put the soap on it ...'

I cup some water in my hands and pour it on to her head, then I rub the soap.

'Now the razor! And be careful!'

It's more difficult with the Gillette razor. I'm trembling a bit. I think of how my mother's blood will flow if I cut her. I hold my breath, then take a big breath, then I'm off, I tilt her head back slightly, then shave, a little bit at a time, starting at her brow and working back towards the neck. A ball of foam full of hair falls on to the floor, making a noise like a great gob of phlegm from the back of someone's throat.

My mother doesn't move, her eyes are closed, she trusts me because so far I haven't cut her.

Now her head is quite bare, just like a woman in mourning. She has a tiny scar by her neck; I never saw it before today.

'I cut myself when I was ten and I was going to the fields with Grandma Henriette, in Louboulou. It was raining and I fell on the back of my head. I'll never know how I managed to fall over like that; I just slipped on a mango stone. I woke up in the pharmacy in the next-door village, Moussanda. Oh well, that's life …'

She runs her hand over her head again, from the front to the back, where the little scar is.

'Well done, I think that's fine! Anyway, my scarf will hide the scar …'

She stands up, takes off the wrap that covered her, while I sweep up around her. She washes her head with water from the bucket. It only takes a few minutes and she goes back into their room.

Ten minutes later she comes out again, dressed in black from head to foot. This time I'm even more surprised:

'Maman, it's too much, even the blind will see we're really in mourning now!'

'So what? Is this house not in mourning?'

Now she looks me up and down in turn.

'What's that you're wearing? You look like a rickshaw boy from Zaire! What have you got on your feet! Honestly, what's Roger been giving you?'

'It's the fashion at school, they're called *Angry Chinas* and—'

'*Angry Chinas!* Well, it's too late to change them now; you'll have to come as you are!'

As she leans forward to pick her bag up off the table her right foot knocks the bucket of water, which I haven't cleared away yet. Fortunately she catches the edge of the table and stops herself falling, but her handbag falls instead. Loose coins roll out and scatter all over the living-room floor, with other things like the lock for the tin trunk she keeps her wraps and important papers in. Her little mirror breaks, just next to the pencils she uses to draw in her eyebrows. The notebook where she and Papa Roger write down the names of the traders who owe her money lands on the other side of the room, but as I go to pick it up something surprising catches my eye, just next to the notebook: a large, brand-new knife, which my mother hurriedly stuffs back into her bag ...

The Bandas

From north to south and from east to west, all the borders are closed. So no one can get to other countries like Cameroon, Gabon, Zaire or Angola, where many traders buy their goods in bulk to sell back home. The few lorries you do see coming into the Grand Marché are only bringing in beef or mutton, because you don't need to travel abroad to buy them, we have them here. On the other side they unload fruit and vegetables, brought from Congolese villages near to Cabinda. For the last few days people have had to buy low quality bananas. They don't come from The Bandas, the village where the best bananas come from, and where Maman Pauline is the only person the peasants will sell to, because she pays cash and doesn't try to confuse them by saying she'll pay half up front then settle the rest next time she's back. She doesn't go down there empty-handed: she offers the peasants packets of cigarettes, toothbrushes, aluminium pots, wraps, salt and sometimes bottles of red wine. The peasants are always pleased to see her, and they give her a warm welcome, as if she was a close family member. I remember going there three times myself. The first time because Maman Pauline wanted to show them she had a child, I was still in primary then; the second time, because the chief of the village hadn't seen me the first time and was a bit cross with my mother, and the third time was last year, when she was showing me and Papa Roger the plot of land the villagers had just given her. I must say, they really spoiled me, the first time, with heaps of presents: a school bag made from sheepskin, a *gris-gris* to protect me from being run over by a car on the way to school, and they made me eat some cat brains because they believe it makes you really clever and clears your mind when you have an exam. And there's more: when I was in The Bandas I had to eat at the house of every peasant who does business with my mother because if I only ate with one of them the others would be sad and say Maman Pauline doesn't love them, or that she loves some more than others. When you're in business you should never upset the suppliers, or their sadness will get mixed up with the goods and no one will want to buy them. So my mother said to me:

'Michel, they're all going to want you to eat with them, and you mustn't say no. You can have a bite here and bite there, just don't eat your fill, and everyone will be happy.'

Inside I was thinking that the problem is when some food is really good, you can't just tell your stomach to wait for the next lot, because if that turns out not to be very nice, you'll wish you'd finished your plate with the family before …

At The Bandas, Maman Pauline always has a big meeting with all the suppliers, in the middle of the village. Each of them tells her how many bunches of bananas they want to sell and the chief of the village fixes a common price by talking to my mother, at a distance from everyone. When they come back to the group, it's all settled, Maman Pauline has slipped the money secretly to the chief, who's all smiles now, and he will hand the money on to the suppliers once my mother's gone. But if you watch carefully, my mother gives a little extra to the chief too, and the peasants don't know about the little extra. That's what puts the smile on the old man's face, why he won't let anyone else come and compete with my mother in the village. The chief is a Vili, and last year he even gave my mother a huge piece of land, just inside the village. Maman Pauline promised him that one day she'd build a big house on the land, and we'd live there, so my mother would be actually on the spot for her merchandise and she could grow her own bananas. For now, though, she's just planted some fruit trees on this sizeable piece of land, and she pays some young villagers to cut back the weeds, otherwise the whole place will turn into bush and we won't be able to find our plot of land.

So today I'm not surprised that no bananas have arrived from The Bandas: to get there you have to take the Micheline, which hasn't been running since the curfew ordered by the Military Committee of the Party, who think bandits often hide out in the villages ...

In the taxi

Maman Pauline didn't speak after we got in the yellow taxi, except when we went round the Kassai roundabout, when I clearly heard her muttering to herself:

'I'll show that northern woman what Pauline Kengué's made of!'

I pretended not to understand.

'What did you say, *Maman*?'

'Nothing ...'

'You said something about the northern woman, and you—'

'If you heard what I said why are you asking me again?'

She looked out of the window at the military truck over-taking us and added:

'God's strange ... how can He accept that a nice man like Kimbouala-Nkaya goes, and we're left with his murderers, who are now celebrating their victory?'

The taxi was travelling slowly, as the town of Pointe-Noire gradually woke up, with passers-by looking like they hadn't slept for three days. I saw Zairian rickshaw boys carrying bricks, beds or fridges, sweating even though the sun hadn't come out yet. There were police at every roundabout but the police seemed to be hanging around doing nothing, not like when they're overrun with traffic jams and keep blowing their whistles. They couldn't complain now that their job's the hardest in the world, in a town with too many second-hand cars and Mobylettes with no brakes or horns.

A lot of the National Popular Army's trucks were leaving the poor neighbourhoods and heading off to the military base near Bloc-55. The soldiers had their guns trained on passers-by, but what people were more afraid of was their dark glasses. I said to myself: The curfew's over, they're going to go and rest for a bit at the military base, then they'll come back to the neighbourhoods after 7 o'clock feeling lively again, to intimidate us some more. I also thought how these soldiers probably had dark glasses because they smoke too much dope and when they've run out they break open the cartridges of their rifles, take out the powder and put it in their coffee, to make it extra strong, so they get really hyped up, as if they'd been drinking Johnnie Walker Red Label, which the black capitalists give their bulldogs to wipe out the pity from their hearts. So the dark glasses are to stop anyone discovering that they're dope heads who execute people just like the animals that got dropped off at the Grand Marché this morning, to be eaten with foufou, manioc and red chilli pepper. Except that the animal killers at the Pointe-Noire slaughter-house don't *have* to smoke dope like the soldiers, because unfortunately everyone agrees that the life of an animal has zero value, it doesn't count, you can kill an animal without being sent to prison.

The reason I'm thinking this about animals is mainly because I'm thinking about Mboua Mabé. How could I have forgotten him, when we bought him here in this market, out of pity, when the wretched dog looked me in the eyes saying, Michel, you're the one I've been waiting for, can I be in your family, you're a good person, with a papa who isn't a huge guy, so isn't scary, and who loves animals as much as human beings? Here, too, is where Mboua Mabé whispered to me that if I let him go with someone else that would be the end of him, and he promised to be really good, he wouldn't bite anyone nice, he wouldn't eat much, and would guard our house as if it was his own kennel and a cat was trying to steal it. I have to remind myself of this, and I don't care if I have to do it a thousand times. Yes, I'm cross with Mboua Mabé because the truth is everything he made me feel, with his doleful look, was just empty words, because when he heard on the radio that Comrade President Marien Ngouabi had been murdered, he ran off like a coward …

At the Grand Marché

We walk to the centre of the tables in the Grand Marché. At every step, traders greet Maman Pauline respectfully and ask her who died in our family, why she's dressed all in black. Then when they see me just behind her, they have to stifle their laughter, because you can't be sad for someone in mourning and at the same time make fun of their child for what he's wearing.

'Pauline, who's died in your family?'

It's the question on everyone's lips. My mother replies that she's in mourning, that for now she doesn't want to talk about it, because she's here for a different reason.

Madame Boudzouna, who's a Bembé like us, starts crying even though she hasn't seen who's dead yet.

'So sad, Pauline! So so sad! Why does the good Lord punish you? You're a good woman, after all!'

Madame Missamou-Miaboumabou, Madame Boudzouna's twin sister, is crying too.

'Pauline, who's died? At least tell us when the burial is, where the funeral's happening! Who's in charge of donations, so my sister and I can pay our dues?'

Madame Augustine Zonza-Tawa, a Lari trader, takes out three crumpled, one-thousand-franc CFA notes and holds them out to me.

'Here, my child, keep that; that's my contribution.'

Maman Pauline gives her back the three crumpled one-thousand-franc notes that I was hoping to stuff into the pocket of my trousers.

She says to Madame Augustine Zonza-Tawa:

'It's all right, Augustine, there's no need for contributions ...'

Mama Nsona-Ndemboukila, another Lari, starts wiping off her lipstick and make-up to make herself less pretty and show that she's sad, like Maman Pauline.

'Pauline, I'll come round to your place this evening, you mustn't be alone, like you've got no friends in this market, or this town! There's more to life than business and money, it's at difficult times like this that you see who's who and who your friends are!'

Within only a few minutes, the word's gone round the Grand Marché that my mother is in mourning, and the group of traders around us starts to grow. I count them, there are now thirty-two of them, all asking questions; no one's taking any notice of me now. Some of them are paying her back money they've owed her for months. Sometimes Maman Pauline takes the money, sometimes she flatly refuses:

'No, Ma Milébé, you've already got four children to feed, your husband died less than two months ago; you can pay something when the time's right, there's no rush ...'

'Pauline, honestly, I can pay you back a hundred per cent, I know you have to buy a coffin, food for the wake, coffee for the whole neighbourhood, etc. Then there's the Pointe-Noire morgue; it costs a lot to keep a body there, all because they make their profit out of other people's misfortunes, and the government doesn't—'

'Don't worry, Ma Milébé, I'll manage ...'

Ma Yvonne Kouloutou-Yabassi roughly shoves aside the other women to get to my mother.

'Come on, out of my way! Let me talk to Pauline! You're tiring her out, twittering like a load of sparrows, and not deciding anything ...'

The tradeswomen move respectfully aside. No one dares contradict Ma Yvonne Kouloutou-Yabassi, she acts like this because she's the oldest and is known as 'Maman la Doyenne'. I've no idea how old she is because she's never changed; I've seen her in the market since I was two years old. Her hair is quite grey, but her face is completely unlined, only her voice reveals that she's perhaps seventy, or more, or less, because at the time she was born birth certificates didn't exist, and when they started doing birth certificates you had to give an age based on how tall you were, or how young, or worn-out you looked. So Maman la Doyenne is one of those people who has 'Born around ...' written on her birth certificate.

Maman la Doyenne is also very well known because she is president of the Association of Women of the Grande Marché. This means she's in charge of the tradeswomen's monthly subscriptions. Out of this money, if one of the tradeswomen loses a family member, they give her something. This is why, having pushed all the other women out of the way, she says proudly to my mother:

'Pauline, the AWGM will pay for all the funeral costs, and when I say all the funeral costs, I mean every last one of them.'

'No, Maman la Doyenne, that's kind of you, but it's OK ...'

And my mother takes Maman la Doyenne to one side. They move two or three metres away from the other tradeswomen, who all peer at them inquisitively, wanting to know what they are saying and why they're not saying it in front of everyone ...'

I want to know too, so I follow them to listen to what they're going to murmur to each other.

My mother goes first:

'Maman la Doyenne, do you know where Antoinette Ebaka is?'

Maman la Doyenne is surprised:

'Is there a problem? Usually on Mondays she comes around nine o'clock because she has a meeting with her colleagues from the Revolutionary Union of Congolese Women.'

Maman Pauline quickly opens her bag and plunges her hand in. She starts rummaging around and I wonder what she's about to do. She's looking for her watch, to see what the time is. She never wears it at the market because there are thieves here with fetishes that allow them to steal watches without their owners noticing.

I'm peering at Maman Pauline's watch too: it's exactly ten past eight and my mother still has to wait almost an hour. It's too much for her, she won't hold out. She turns back and yells at the women who are staring at her back there:

'Listen to me, I'm going to go and wait opposite, at Chez Gaspard's. If anyone sees Antoinette Ebaka, tell her I'm waiting for her there and I've got better things to do!'

The tradeswomen all start talking then they scatter. Each one goes back to her own table; they probably don't want their names mixed up in this business.

Maman la Doyenne says to my mother:

'Don't go to the café now, Pauline ...'

'Why not? Is there a rule against it?'

'I'm older than you; I could be your mother too. It's a word of advice, Pauline, just listen to me. Looking at you, you don't seem like the Pauline Kengué I know ...'

Maman Pauline isn't listening to her. She tightens her black scarf round her head, adjusts her wrap round her waist, looks at me as if to say it's time to leave the market, it's filling up steadily, as if people are just leading their normal lives and have forgotten that the body of Comrade President Marien Ngouabi hasn't been buried yet. I was convinced that the soldiers went back to their base in the morning, then returned to keep watch during the curfew from seven o'clock onwards, so I'm amazed to see hundreds of other fresh-looking troops getting out of trucks and mingling with the crowd in the market. Some people stand aside for them to pass, others run off like thieves. The soldiers are armed to the teeth, with dark glasses just like the ones I saw earlier when I was in the yellow taxi. They move about in groups, pointing at the crowds, stopping people at random, saying it's a check for the market's security. Sometimes they ask for identity cards and call people by their first names when they ask questions.

'It's a routine check … Do you have family in Brazzaville? Do you have a family member in the army? What ethnic group are you?'

I think to myself that my mother isn't going to be able to get too cross with this Antoinette Ebaka woman, because of her title as 'leader of the Revolutionary Union of Congolese Women of the Grand Marché'; if there's a problem the soldiers will say the northern woman's right and my mother's a bad woman, because she's a southerner.

This is the moment to put a stop to it.

'Let's go home, *Maman*.'

'What did you say?'

'We'd better go home, *Maman*.'

She takes out a ten-thousand-franc CFA note from her bag. Her face is shut off, her eyes all red.

'Take this money! You're about as brave as a wet turkey. Get a yellow taxi, go home to Voungou; Captain Kimbouala-Nkaya will be really proud of you in the world beyond!'

'But, *Maman*, I—'

'Just go! I can deal with this on my own!'

I don't take the note, and I don't move. She puts the money back in her bag and starts walking out of the market.

I don't know what to do, so I stay put, then I start moving, with my eyes on Maman Pauline, who is still walking.

As I'm walking, I run into an old man selling dogs. There are twenty or more of them, and they're fighting over the food the seller's giving them. I go up very close; one of them looks really like Mboua Mabé.

'Mboua Mabé! Mboua Mabé! Mboua Mabé!' I yell.

The dog in question pricks up his ears and wags his tail. He has those eyes, the ones that stared at me, and I remember too it was exactly here that Papa Roger and I bought Mboua Mabé! Yes, it's him. There's no mistaking him. When he looks straight at me it sends shivers down my spine and my hair stands on end. Mboua Mabé is here! He's come back to where he started! But it's too late, I'm over him already. Anyway, I have no money to buy him off the old man. Even if Papa Roger had been with me and I'd begged him to buy Mboua Mabé, he'd say that's enough, he'd already done his bit. So I carry on walking, I turn my back on the dog, who's now howling like a coyote.

A man jostles me and cackles:

'Hey, little one, your armband there cracks me up! Who are you, the secret son of Comrade President Marien Ngouabi, or what?'

Several people join him, surrounding me and laughing loudly. Down the far end I can even see some soldiers, who should be looking sad, laughing at me, instead of congratulating me for being a true fanatic for our leader of the Revolution.

I run off like a papaya thief. My *Angry Chinas* help a lot, as my feet are light and I jump, pivoting to the left, then to the right. I don't care that people are still laughing at me, they move out of the way anyway because they actually think there's something not right in my head.

I keep going straight, and arrive at the last tables in the market. From here I can see Maman Pauline, who has just arrived at the drink stand, Chez Gaspard ...

Chez Gaspard

I'm standing panting behind Maman Pauline, who's looking into the interior of Chez Gaspard. There are over a hundred women in there and they're all dressed in bright red wrappers, the colour of our national flag, and on their wrappers it says 'Revolutionary Union of Congolese Women', with the head of Comrade President Marien Ngouabi and his black wife Céline Ngouabi. I'm glad what I'm wearing isn't this colour, or people would think I'm a woman who wants to join the group too.

So this is where they hold the meeting Maman la Doyenne was talking about. She knew Antoinette Ebaka was in the bar, but she didn't want to tell my mother, because she didn't want to get involved in other people's problems. It's her age that has brought her this wisdom, and I think she's a hundred per cent right, because old mamas are never wrong, they can sniff out trouble from a distance, or even further …

Maman Pauline yells at the top of her voice:

'Where are you hiding, Antoinette? Show yourself if you're brave enough!'

The women of the Revolutionary Union all turn round and look over at the entrance to the bar. They are all struck at once by my mother's black outfit, which is even more noticeable against all this red. The silence lasts at most thirty seconds, but it feels like no one here has spoken for an hour or more, till suddenly something falls to the ground, it sounds like several glasses breaking. The waitress has dropped the tray and is staring open mouthed at Maman Pauline, swinging her head back and forth between my mother and a woman sitting right at the back, surrounded by other women. I realise at once this must be the famous Antoinette Ebaka. She's very muscly; she looks like she spends her days unloading sacks of cement at Pointe-Noire docks. Her jaws look like the fuel tank on a Vélo-SoleX and her hair is cut very short, like those men who ask the barber to use a Gillette razor to trace a line from their brow to the middle of the head ...

The woman answers:

'I'm here, Pauline. We're holding a very important meeting, as you can see. If it's about the money I owe you I can—'

Maman Pauline doesn't wait for her to finish her sentence, she strides over to Antoinette Ebaka, her hand raised high above her head. And when the other women see the blade of the long knife glinting in the sunlight they all start screaming, crying for help and running in all directions, while I try to catch hold of Maman Pauline. It's too late, though, I'm too late – she has already dealt the first blow, another one's coming now ...

113 Avenue Linguissi-Tchicaya

I run like a madman, right through the Grand Marché neighbourhood.

I've never run this fast. When I overtake people I look back without stopping, and they're already way behind me. That's when I realise I'm running really really fast.

Sometimes I hear people burst out laughing behind me. Maybe they're laughing at my outfit, or at the way I'm running, a bit lopsided, a bit stooped, like a hunchback ...

I turn down a little side street with no name and find myself in the yard of a family who are outside eating. It's a gathering: there are at least forty people here, staring at me with huge eyes before they begin to shout at me, and throw spoons and forks, which I duck to avoid as best I can.

'Idiot! Thief!'

They think I'm one of the thieves from the Grand Marché who dash across their plot almost every day.

Sweat is dripping down into my eyes. I wipe my brow with my right wrist, I don't stop. In fact, I keep going – faster.

I'm in Avenue Paillet now, and several police cars pass me going the other way, towards the market. The sirens and flashing lights force cars to move aside and let them pass at breakneck speed.

But they'll be too late. They don't know Maman Pauline

has already been taken away, not by a police car but by a truck full of soldiers.

As the cars go past I bounce around on the spot, like I'm jogging.

The last one has just disappeared, and I decide to turn off right, towards the Avenue Moé-Kaat-Matou.

I grit my teeth, my back still hunched. I accelerate.

This avenue's quieter than the Avenue Paillet with banks and expensive restaurants that only whites and black capitalists go to. I'm not going to slow down just because it's quiet here! No way!

I get to the Boulevard Charles-de-Gaulle. I need to find the Avenue Agostino-Neto, Papa Roger's explained it to me, and I think it's about three hundred metres further down, on my right.

I notice a military truck coming towards me. I slow down, act like I'm going somewhere and I'm looking for the street name. The truck draws level with me. I'm sure it's going to stop, they'll ask me what I'm doing in this neighbourhood and why I'm running like I've stolen something. I hear the noise of guns – Click! Click! Click! I can see them pointing at me now. I close my eyes. But suddenly I hear laughter: my armband! The soldiers have worked out that I'm a true fan of Comrade Marien Ngouabi. They're saluting me now, then the truck accelerates off in the direction of the Grand Marché.

I'm panting. I'm trembling. If they knew who I was and what has just happened at the Grand Marché they'd pick me up at once …

I set off running again.

Yes, running.

I must get there in time. I follow the direction of the military truck they've loaded Maman Pauline into like a sack of potatoes. But the truck disappeared ages ago, between the moment I went to phone Papa Roger from the Post Office and the moment he says:

'Go the way the truck went; I'm sure it'll be going to 113 Avenue Linguissi-Tchicaya. Wait for me there ...'

I know the soldiers in the truck will be roughing up my mother. What's at 113 Avenue Linguissi-Tchicaya? I've never heard of this address before. Papa Roger said:

'It's in Mpita, near the Côte Sauvage and the whites' cemetery.'

I've never been there, but I have heard strange tales about what goes on near the Côte Sauvage: sorcerers making their gris-gris on the beach at four in the morning, bodies floating on the water, albinos sacrificed and found cut into pieces ...

The truck Maman Pauline's been taken away in, heading for Mpita, was like the ones you see in our neighbourhood: black, with a bright red hood, like our revolutionary flag. The windows are smoked glass; I couldn't make out the face of the driver or the men sitting beside him. In the back, soldiers were shouting for joy. I recalled how they had dragged Maman Pauline along the ground, ripping her clothes, how she was already unconscious, unaware they were throwing her inside a truck, full of armed men who'd probably been smoking cannabis all night to keep awake during the curfew.

The soldiers won't go easy on her. My mother is beautiful, she's young. Men turn round in the street to look at her. Papa Roger gets jealous if someone says his wife is pretty.

Yes, my mother is very beautiful and young, and that makes me really afraid.

But I won't think about it.

I need to wipe it from my mind, just listen to what Papa Roger said, even if I've lost sight of the military truck.

'Go the way the truck went; I'm sure it'll be going to 113, Avenue Linguissi-Tchicaya. Wait for me there ...'

As I run I start to smell the Atlantic Ocean, and it's like being really small again. Maman Pauline's holding my hand, we're walking down the Avenue of Independence to go and see Uncle Albert Moukila. She tells me to behave nicely, to answer all my uncle's questions. I promise I'll be the smartest kid in the whole of Pointe-Noire, in the Congo, even, and maybe in the whole of Africa. She laughs and says it's fine if I'm just the smartest kid in the neighbourhood.

'Before you fight the big battles, son, you have to win the little ones ...'

She tells me about her village, Louboulou, which was ruled by Grandpa Massengo. She's the last but one child of Grandma Henriette Nsoko, just before Uncle Mompéro, the carpenter. But Grandpa Massengo had so many children and wives that we're practically related to the whole village, and if you aren't careful you can find yourself marrying a relative, and your descendants will be deformed. She grew up there, till she got together with a policeman from Mouyondzi, who ran off the day I came into the world. I have never seen this policeman.

Maman Pauline packed her bags for Pointe-Noire. Uncle René met her. He helped her to set up her peanut business in the Grand Marché. Here she met a man, a small, kind man, who was already married: Papa Roger ...

She tells me something she's often said before: if she hadn't met Papa Roger, she and I would have been well and truly screwed. So Papa Roger is a spirit sent from heaven: he already had a wife, lots of children, but he accepted Maman Pauline and the boy who wasn't his.

My mother isn't sad now, not like she was before she found me some brothers and sisters. That's life, she says. Some people can have lots, some people are just put on this earth to have one, even with all the fetishes in the world, they'll never have another.

We're still walking, and she keeps on and on:

'Always do your school work.'

'Always be in the top five in the class.'

'Hey, *Maman*, I want to be top!'

She smiles and says again:

'I just told you, son: before you take on the big battles, win the little ones …'

Then she wipes the dust off my plastic sandals.

'Your uncle Albert doesn't like dirt, and he sees everything, like through a magnifying glass …'

She stops and buys dumplings and Beninese soup. It's for my cousins: Magicien and his twin sister Bienvenue, and for their big brothers, Abeille, Djoudjou and Firmin. They'll all be happy to see Maman Pauline. Because my mother spoils them. She always gives them a bit of money when she leaves. And they all chorus:

'Thank you, Papa Pauline …'

They call her 'Papa Pauline' because she is their aunt, so their father's sister, so she's like their 'papa' too, even if she's a woman. They can't say 'Maman Pauline' like me because she's not their mother. 'Papa Pauline' is better, and it's right. 'Tata Pauline' or 'Auntie Pauline' sounds too distant, they don't like that. They say Maman Pauline is their lady papa.

I wander through Mpita with the image of my mother in my head.

I'm on Avenue Moe-Telli now; I cross it in under a minute, my heart's got used to going flat out.

I can't feel my breathing.

I'm like a machine with brand-new batteries.

I see the names of the Avenues pass by: Moé-Vangoula; then Barthélemy-Boganda, which later turns into Emerald Avenue, which feeds into the famous Avenue Linguissi-Tchicaya.

I walk up it, and when I get to number 113 I raise my head and read on a big black sign:

POINTE-NOIRE JAIL

White cranes never die

Pointe-Noire jail is three kilometres from the Grand Marché, next to the Compagnie Territorial Police Force in Mpita, where I've never set foot till now.

When Papa Roger and Uncle René meet me outside the entrance, I try to hide my eyes, which are swollen with crying that started when the soldiers took Maman Pauline away in handcuffs, with the whole market watching, like it was an entertainment.

I'd managed to run off and find my way to the Post Office and make a reverse-charge call to Papa Roger, who phoned Uncle René at once and told me to start running, not to look back, and to wait for him at 113 Avenue Linguissi-Tchicaya ...

Uncle René and Papa Roger walk into the jail and go up to an old policeman who's on reception, behind some bars. It's very busy, but when Uncle René comes through, people stand aside, because they sense at once that he's important, just from the way he walks, in his well-pressed trousers.

You have to raise your voice really loud to talk to the old policeman on reception; he answers through a microphone, and tells you to go and take a ticket at the back of the room, leave your identity card and wait till someone calls you. He doesn't even look up when he tells Uncle René to go and take a ticket. My uncle gives three little taps on the bars, the old policeman looks at him, he notices the Congolese Party of Labour membership card my uncle's just taken out. The old policeman stands to attention; you'd think Uncle René was a colonel or a general in the National Popular Army.

'At your service, comrade party member!'

'You're a Bembé, aren't you?'

The old policeman likes this.

'How did you know that, comrade party member?'

'Your accent, it's the same as where I come from: Bouenza ...'

My uncle speaks to him directly in Bembé; he doesn't want the people waiting for their turn to hear what's being said. I don't speak Bembé very fluently, but I understand what's being said.

Uncle René asks him to take us to his boss's office. The old policeman suddenly changes his manner.

'Oh no, comrade party member, the boss won't be able to see you today, there's been a serious problem over at the Grand Marché, he's waiting for someone—'

'I know, he's waiting for me, René Mabahou, we spoke on the phone a couple of hours ago ...'

The old policeman goes over to talk to his colleague, who is sitting behind him, at the back, reading through a mountain of papers, his face completely hidden by smoke from the cigarette stuck in his mouth. The two policemen have a talk, look across at us, then talk some more, and his colleague comes to take the place of the old man, who leaves the cage, comes round to us, and tells us to follow him.

We go down a long corridor, the old policeman first, followed by Uncle René, Papa Roger, and last of all me. Our footsteps echo as we walk. The corridors here are like in a hospital, the walls are white, it smells of medicine, or maybe I'm imagining it.

At the end of the corridor, you turn right, the old police-man opens a door and closes it again behind us. We go up some more stairs, till we reach the third floor and the old policeman's panting as he says:

'Here we are …'

We're standing at a door that has four locks. The old police-man presses a red button three times. A noise comes from the first lock, then the second, then the third, then the fourth, and when the door opens we see the head of another old police-man, though not so old as the one in charge of us. The old one talks quietly to the not-quite-so-old one, the not-quite-so-old one peers closely at our faces, pulls a disgusted face , and tells us to go in, closing the door quickly behind us, while the old policeman goes back to his cage again.

The air-conditioning's too high; we'll die of cold if we have to wait long. On the wall to my left there's a portrait of Comrade President Marien Ngouabi level with me. The same one's in Ma Moubobi's shop, only this one's ten times bigger, if you look at it too hard you'll start to think Comrade President Marien Ngouabi isn't dead, he's just pretended to disappear, to make everyone love him more, now and for ever.

Uncle René paces around, looking at his watch.

The door next to him has just opened and a nasty-looking lady says:

'You may come in …'

My father and my uncle hurry inside and when I get to the door the woman shakes her head.

'You'll have to wait here …'

Papa Roger turns around, he's angry with the woman.

'We're going to talk about his mother in there, why does he have to wait here?'

'Because he's a minor, and—'

'Nadège, let the boy come in, he was there when it happened ...'

The voice comes from behind the nasty lady, belonging to a small, bald gentleman.

So in I go too ...

This room is almost like a large house, and it's a shame to waste so much space on an office for a small, bald gentleman. From the two large windows in the office you can see what's happening down in the yard and in the road, where every car is being searched by policemen.

It's hard to believe, when you're in an office like this, that in the buildings next door they're holding thieves, bandits, delinquents and the most dangerous criminals in the whole of Pointe-Noire.

In the middle of the office there's a round table made of wood, with fifteen chairs – I've just counted.

We sit down, with Uncle René right opposite the small, bald gentleman, my father to the right of my uncle, and me to his left.

The small, bald gentleman starts by addressing Papa Roger and me:

'For those who don't know me, I am Donatien Mabiala, Deputy Director of the Penal Service ...'

He tightens and adjusts his tie.

'Comrade party member René Mabahou called me and requested a meeting with me regarding a serious attempted murder which took place late this morning, at the Grand Marché. Exceptionally, I agreed to the meeting, because comrade party member René Mabahou told me a little about what was happening regarding his sister, who is now being held in the building opposite ...'

He pauses for a long breath and adjusts his tie again.

'I know comrade party member René Mabahou, we used to run into each other at meetings of the regional section of the Congolese Party of Labour. I have no reason not to take his word, but in this case it's not a question of words but of a coldly calculated act, perpetrated with the intent of taking the life of someone who is currently hospitalised at Adolphe-Cissé, and seriously wounded. Obviously there are likely to be extremely serious consequences; it's best I warn you now. But I also promised comrade party member René Mabahou, in the light of all he has done for the Congolese Socialist Revolution, that I would do anything I could to help him, though naturally only within the limits of my means, which are modest ...'

Uncle René nods, to say thank you, and the deputy director continues:

'You will be aware, as I am, that this incident has occurred at the wrong moment, and appears to have – how shall I put it? – *political* implications. Madame Pauline Kengué, by her own admission, is apparently the sister of Captain Kimbouala-Nkaya. My dear René, while I have every respect for your status as a member of the Congolese Party of Labour, that just won't wash unless you are prepared to formally confirm what you said to me on the telephone in the presence of Jean-Pierre Oko-Bankala, the examining magistrate, who has been asked by our provisional government, which is obviously already aware of the tragedy and is following the case very closely, on account of its sensitive nature, to proceed promptly and rapidly to apply the appropriate sanctions ...'

Suddenly we hear a door opening behind us. Papa Roger, Uncle René and I all turn round: an extremely tall, thin man has entered the office. He doesn't acknowledge anyone, just sits down next to the director who says:

'Allow me to present the examining magistrate, Jean-Pierre Oko-Bankala ...'

The man crosses his legs and opens a large blue book. He has a red Biro in his left hand and a black Biro in his right hand.

'I would not normally hold a little meeting like this, but Deputy Director Donatien Mabiala is a friend, and he has assured me that this business is simply a misunderstanding, but I'd like to be sure that's true, I'd like to hear it directly from the family, before deciding what course of action I should take ...'

When he talks, his voice is very deep, like someone who smokes all day.

He crosses his legs, this time the other way, and looks Uncle René straight in the eye.

'Monsieur Mabahou, either I can put a red line through this affair, here and now, or with a stroke of this black pen I can put your sister behind bars for many, many years ...'

My uncle replies:

'Sir, I think we are conscious of the difficulty of your task in these dark days of our national history, and we are here to try to find a solution ...'

'Splendid! I will ask you to be sincere with me, since I have the feeling this is no simple matter of common law, more a question of National Security ...'

He plays with the black pen and asks:

'Monsieur René Mabahou, answer me clearly, look me straight in the eye, and as your soul and your conscience are your witness: is Captain Kimbouala-Nkaya your brother, and therefore also the brother of Pauline Kengué, as the latter declared at the moment of her arrest in the Grand Marché, and continues to affirm even now, in her cell?'

Uncle René avoids looking at Judge Oko-Bankala and replies:

'No, Captain Kimbouala-Nkaya is not the brother of my sister Pauline Kengué, and he's not my brother either …'

Judge Oko-Bankala plays with the red Biro.

'So you've never set eyes on him?'

Uncle René still doesn't look at him.

'No, sir, I've never set eyes on him in my life …'

'You're not looking at me, sir!'

'That's because I'm thinking …'

Judge Oko-Bankala puts the two pens down on the table, and addresses Deputy Director Donatien Mabiala:

'We had cases like this before … I wouldn't be surprised if Madame Pauline Kengué turned out to be a compulsive liar, suffering from a delusional and obsessive compulsion to claim relatedness to someone she has never known and never met …'

Papa Roger doesn't like this.

'I won't have Pauline called a compulsive liar and all those other things you said, and what's more I—'

'Roger!' interrupts Uncle René.

And I'm thinking: Why doesn't Judge Oko-Bankala ask me if Captain Kimbouala-Nkaya was my uncle? Because I'll tell him the truth, I'll tell him a thousand times over what I've already said here: that Captain Kimbouala-Nkaya is definitely my uncle, that we went to his house and we ate so well there that I told my mother I'd like to stay in Brazzaville for the rest of my life so I can always eat pig when my uncle has guests in his fine, brick-built house. Yes, if he asks me I'll tell Judge Oko-Bankala how kind my Uncle Kimbouala-Nkaya was, that he didn't talk much, but he let me try his military beret on in front of the mirror in the living room, striking military poses and shouting, 'Atten-shun!' I would also say that Uncle Kimbouala-Nkaya being so kind didn't mean you took advantage of his kindness, and his children and I all knew that you weren't allowed to touch the gun he kept hidden in his office. I'll tell Judge Oko-Bankala, too, that the first time I watched television was at Uncle Kimbouala-Nkaya's house, when Muhammad Ali and George Foreman had their fight in Kinshasa at the 20th May Stadium, and we jumped for joy and yelled: 'Ali, *boma yé!* Ali, *boma yé!* Ali, *boma yé!*' And if Judge Oka-Bankala still doesn't believe I'm telling the truth, if he thinks I'm a compulsive liar too, or whatever else he says I am, I'll just tell him some more about my uncle's house, how fine it was, even if it wasn't finished, and how everyone in the Plateau des Quinze-Ans neighbourhood envied it. I'll tell him how before you get to the inner courtyard you have to go down a long corridor and every so often along this corridor there are rooms that any member of the family who turns up in Brazzaville can stay in. Once you've gone down the corridor and reached the circular courtyard the light comes in from above because there's no roof. And there, too, all the way round the circular courtyard, Uncle Kimbouala-Nkaya built four apartments and the one he lives in with his wife is the one facing you, the biggest and brightest of all. From outside you might think it's a little room, but inside there's a big dining room, a shower, like in the Victory Palace Hotel, and toilets, like in the Victory Palace Hotel, and you have to watch out because once you've finished what you have to do, you pull on a chain so the water will flush out what comes out of your belly, and I'm not going to describe that to Judge Oko-Bankala or he'll say I exaggerate and sometimes I say rude things without meaning to. I'll tell him all that, because when I think about everything that's happened—

'Hello? Are you listening to me or are you daydreaming, boy?'

Judge Oko-Bankala's speaking to me! He's speaking to me, Michel!

'Come on, boy, I've just asked you the same question three times, but your mind's somewhere else. I'll ask you again: was Captain Kimbouala-Nkaya your uncle?'

I look at Uncle René's face, then over at my father, who suddenly lowers his gaze. Papa Roger has never lowered his gaze like that with me. I usually look down first.

The judge plays with the black Biro and I remember that means he can send Maman Pauline to prison for many, many years, because he works for the Military Committee of the Party.

I think of Uncle Kimbouala-Nkaya: if I betray him he'll think I'm a coward, and the poor captain will not sleep easy up there, because of me.

But then I think of Maman Pauline, and I ask myself: If she was me, Michel, and I was Maman Pauline, how would she answer Judge Oko-Bankala? I'm sure that if she was me, Michel, she would say to herself: Michel, this is your chance to show you're a man, to choose to express what's in your heart, what's good and true. That's the voice you need to listen to.

'Come on, boy, this is the last time I'll ask you the question, I've got better things to do: was Captain Kimbouala-Nkaya the brother of your mother – that is to say, your uncle?'

I let the little voice inside me speak up and I say:

'Captain Kimbouala-Nkaya was not my uncle, but he's a white crane now, and white cranes never die ...'

ABOUT THE AUTHOR

Alain Mabanckou was born in Congo in 1966. An award-winning novelist, poet, and essayist, Mabanckou currently lives in Los Angeles, where he teaches literature at UCLA. He is the author of *African Psycho, Broken Glass, Black Bazaar,* and *Tomorrow I'll Be Twenty,* as well as *The Lights of Pointe-Noire* and *Black Moses* (both published by The New Press). In 2015, Mabanckou was a finalist for the Man Booker International Prize.

ABOUT THE TRANSLATOR

Helen Stevenson is a translator who lives in Somerset, England. She has translated works by Marie Darrieussecq, Alice Ferney, and Catherine Millet, as well as several books by Alain Mabanckou. Her translation of Mabanckou's *The Lights of Pointe-Noire* won the Grand Prix, 2015 French Voices Award.

PUBLISHING IN THE PUBLIC INTEREST

Thank you for reading this book published by The New Press. The New Press is a nonprofit, public interest publisher. New Press books and authors play a crucial role in sparking conversations about the key political and social issues of our day.

We hope you enjoyed this book and that you will stay in touch with The New Press. Here are a few ways to stay up to date with our books, events, and the issues we cover:

- Sign up at www.thenewpress.com/subscribe to receive updates on New Press authors and issues and to be notified about local events
- Like us on Facebook: www.facebook.com /newpressbooks
- Follow us on Twitter: www.twitter.com /thenewpress

Please consider buying New Press books for yourself; for friends and family; or to donate to schools, libraries, community centers, prison libraries, and other organizations involved with the issues our authors write about.

The New Press is a 501(c)(3) nonprofit organization. You can also support our work with a tax-deductible gift by visiting www.thenewpress.com/donate.